HAVING THE TIME OF MY MIDLIFE

GOOD TO THE LAST DEATH

BOOK 12

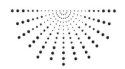

ROBYN PETERMAN

ACKNOWLEDGMENTS

The Good To The Last Death Series is a pleasure to write. *Having the Time of My Midlife* was a joy and an obsession for me. Telling stories is my passion and my passion has been fulfilled with this series. Daisy, Gideon and the gang bring me an absurd amount of joy and I hope you feel the same way. See some old friends and meet some new ones!

As always, writing may be a solitary sport, but it takes a whole bunch of people to make the magic happen.

Renee — Thank you for my beautiful cover and for being the best badass critique partner in the world. TMB. LOL

Wanda — You are the freaking bomb. Love you to the moon and back.

Heather, Nancy, Caroline and Wanda — Thank you for reading early and helping me find the booboos. You all rock.

My Readers — Thank you for loving the stories that come from my warped mind. It thrills me.

Steve, Henry and Audrey — Your love and support makes all of this so much more fun. I love you people endlessly.

DEDICATION

For Jessica. You make these books come to life! Love you!

BOOK DESCRIPTION

HAVING THE TIME OF MY MIDLIFE

Midlife is madness and the crisis is expensive... to my sanity.

Just when I think everything is calming down, it ramps back up to eleven. On what should be one of the happiest and most romantic days of my life, the unthinkable happens.

The ghosts I'd so kindly guided into the Light showed up on my front porch, including my dead husband.

Something or someone is messing with the balance and if it's not remedied, the Darkness will destroy the world.

I really don't have time for that crap.

With the love of my Immortal life and my batsh*t crazy friends by my side, I'll take on the Higher Power and show It a thing or two; like what true faith means. No one is going to play life and death games with me. If they do... they'll lose.

Wish me luck, because this time next week, I plan to be having the time of my midlife.

CHAPTER ONE

I STOOD ON THE FRONT PORCH OF THE HOUSE GIDEON AND I HAD created together with love and gazed out over the yard in shock. My tummy flipped, but it wasn't from fear or stress. It was from giddiness and joy. Normally, the yard was grass and trees. Today, it was not.

Someone, or a bunch of someones, had converted our property into an exquisite garden. It was pure magic. Candles hung overhead in the air, floating on a gentle and fragrant breeze. Scattered peach and pale-pink rose petals created a path leading to a gazebo covered in vines bursting with white, cream, and dusty rose-colored blossoms. Flowers and ornamental grasses swayed in the light wind while the clouds in the sky appeared larger and puffier. Flocks of wildly colored birds darted in and out of the trees, and the winter sun bathed the entire picture in a warm golden glow. For it being the middle of winter, it was impressive.

"Oh my," I whispered, taking it all in with delight. June had given me some solid advice ten minutes earlier as I'd waited in the foyer for my surprise wedding to begin.

"Once the dress is on, don't worry about it getting messed up," she said sagely. "It will at some point and who cares? Listen to the ceremony, and don't get wasted at the reception."

They were logical and smart pointers, just like my buddy June. I added one more thought to the list—take in the beauty around me and treasure it.

"You look so lovely, Daisy girl," Gram said as she hovered next to me in all her ghostly glory. "Lemme tell you, I'm so dang excited to walk my baby down the aisle, I think my head might fall off! Kiddin'!" she added to my relief. Having to superglue Gram's head back on during the wedding march might kill some of the romantic atmosphere. The old ghost chuckled and then gazed at me fondly. "You bein' happy just dills my pickles. You look as fine as a frog hair split four ways."

I giggled. Gram was being vintage Gram. "I love you and thank you."

"For what?" she asked, caressing my cheek with her papery and transparent hand.

"For loving me. For raising me. For staying with me," I said, pulling out a tissue and putting it to good use. "And for walking me down the aisle."

"Pleasure is all mine, baby girl," she told me. "All mine."

Dabbing at my eyes so I didn't have a streaky, tear-stained face, I gazed at the stunning picture in front of me. There were several rows of seating. Everyone was here—Heather and Missy held hands and leaned into each other the way people who loved each other did. Tim, Jennifer, June and Charlie sat together. June held a sleepy Alana Catherine on her lap, and my fur babies, Donna and Karen, lay on the ground at her feet. Charlie's arm was draped over June's shoulders, and Jennifer, with a bottle of wine in hand, cooed at my baby. As my friend liked to say… it was five o'clock somewhere. Tim, dapper in his mail uniform, had added a bow tie and a top hat to his look. It was a massive fashion faux pas—so wrong it was absolutely right. Instead of a notebook and pen, today, my socially awkward buddy had a camera and was snapping pictures. I knew this day would stay in my heart and my memories, but it would be lovely to have physical reminders.

My newest friends, Zander and his sister Catriona, sat with my Angel siblings—Rafe, Gabe, Abby and Prue. Tory and Amelia rounded out the group. Amelia sat next to Rafe, and their connection was undeniable. The energy around them was electric. Everyone was dressed to the nines and looked like they'd stepped off the cover of a magazine. Zander couldn't take his eyes off Prue. She studiously ignored him, of course, but the small smile pulling at her lips was a dead giveaway that she was into it. There was a story developing there, and I had my fingers crossed for a happily ever after. However, the biggest story of that grouping was Gabe and Tory. Tory no longer denied her feelings for my brother. They were taking it slow, but they had an eternity to get it right. Both of them were glowing… literally.

Their love story had been thousands of years in the making, and I had a feeling it was about to unfold into a beautiful ending.

"It's almost time," Gram said softly. "You ready?"

"More ready than I've ever been," I told her with a smile so wide it hurt my cheeks. "Where's Gideon?"

"He'll be coming out with Candy Vargo in just a sec," she told me. "That boy has it bad for you. He's been walking around grinnin' like a possum eatin' a sweet tater!"

"That makes two of us," I said with a laugh.

The Four Horsemen of the Apocalypse in full-on glittering drag were running the show. Dirk seated the last of the guests. Wally coordinated all the music—which was kind of alarming, considering the playlist, but nothing would ruin this day, even cringy inappropriate songs. Fred traipsed up and down the aisle, offering flutes of champagne. Most everyone accepted a glass. Jennifer took two. Carl stood next to the gazebo, looking fabulous, and posed for the camera. Tim obliged and took plenty of pics.

Mr. Jackson and my three hundred or so other dead guests were in attendance as well. They might have been more excited about the ceremony than I was. The ghosts darted around and chattered with rabid excitement. There were a few random body parts lying around. Didn't matter. It was par for the course in my life, and I'd deal with it and superglue them back together after the ceremony. It was macabre, beautiful and very, very right. I wore many hats... mom, soon-to-be wife, sister, granddaughter, friend, Angel of Mercy, badass, and Death Counselor. It was perfect that all my people were here.

Candy Vargo appeared on the platform of the gazebo in a blast of sparkling orange mist. The guests applauded her showmanship. She bowed and tossed boxes of toothpicks to the crowd. I almost choked on my spit at the outfit she wore. She had on a magnificent gold Prada sheath dress that was simple in design and gorgeous in reality. Of course, she paired it with shitty tennis shoes and a toothpick hanging out of her mouth, but Candy was Candy, and that wasn't ever going to change. The queens had dressed her—everything except the shoes and the toothpick accessory. I was sure of that. When her gaze met mine, she smiled, waved, and then flipped me off.

I returned the gesture, and she cackled like an idiot.

4

"You ready, asshead?" she yelled.

"I'm ready, butthole," I yelled back.

"Then let's get this fuckin' party started!"

"Watch that mouth," Gram told her, giving her the stink-eye.

The Keeper of Fate blanched and gave Gram a thumbs up. I didn't believe Candy Vargo was capable of watching her mouth. Honestly, I didn't want her to. It wouldn't be a party without Candy dropping a few F-bombs.

"Oh my!" Dirk squealed as Gideon walked onto the gazebo. "You are hotter than Satan's underpants—if he existed—which he doesn't, but I'm sticking with my story!"

Dirk was correct. My heart skipped a beat, and my mouth went dry when our eyes met. The man of my dreams gazed at me with love and desire in his eyes. It made me forget for a moment that we weren't the only people here. It was humbling to the point that I thought I might faint. The smile pulling at the corner of his kissable lips promised a lifetime of adventure. I was all in.

"All right, people," Candy shouted. "Get your asses up. You gotta stand when the bride walks down the aisle."

The people listened.

"Lookin' like it's our turn," Gram said.

"Lookin' like it is," I agreed.

"Music," Candy Vargo ordered, pointing her chewed-up toothpick at Wally.

"On it, Doll Face!" Wally pushed the button, and Sting's voice came through the speakers. *Every Breath You Take* blasted loud and proud.

A few of the guests winced at the song choice, but I just shook my head and went with it. Nothing could ruin my day. I would have loved for my mom and dad to be here, but that wasn't possible. I was thrilled with the gathering assembled. It included my nearest and dearest.

The melody of the song was beautiful, even if the words were kind of creepy. I felt the strong impulse to run to Gideon, tackle him and play tonsil hockey, but thankfully, Gram had tucked her ghostly arm through mine. Literally. She floated at a slower pace, which was far more appropriate. It would have been a major faux pas for me to sprint down the aisle dragging my dead grandmother, but it was exactly what I wanted to do.

Gideon's eyes burned red with love and adoration as I approached. Gram handed me over and booped the Grim Reaper's nose before she floated away, seating herself next to Heather and Missy.

"Stunning," Gideon whispered.

"Back at ya, Sexy Pants," I said. "You okay with this? I mean, it seems kind of shotgun."

He threw his head back and laughed. It filled my soul.

Gideon in a tux should be illegal. He was more beautiful than any movie star or model from a magazine. But even more important than his fine abs, ass, kissable lips and other things I shouldn't think about while our families, friends and daughter were present was his heart. It was kind, strong, loving and good. And it was mine.

"It's my fuckin' turn," Candy Vargo announced, pulling out a toothpick box that she had turned into a cheat sheet.

"Let's try to keep the profanity to a minimum," Tim suggested.

"Will do. Jackasses, did you hear the mailman?" she demanded of Gideon and me with a cackle.

"Pretty sure he was talking to you," I shot back.

"Hmm…" She considered the possibility and then shrugged. "You ready for me to marry you two?"

"Do we have a choice?" I asked with an answering grin.

"Nope."

"Then we're ready," Gideon said.

"Did either of you happen to write your fuckin' vows?" Candy Vargo inquired.

"Watch that mouth, girlie, or I'm gonna tie your tongue in a knot," Gram shouted.

"My bad," Candy answered her with a wave. She refocused on us. "So? Vows?"

I squinted at her in disbelief. "Are you serious? Neither one of us even knew we were getting married this afternoon. Why would you think we'd have written our own vows?

"Relax your fuckin' sphincter crack," Candy said. "You can just pull 'em out of your ass."

"Candy Vargo," Gram called out, waggling her finger.

"Whoops," Candy said. "I meant to say, relax your fornicating gluteal muscles."

"Lordy, have mercy," Gram choked out a laugh. "I ain't sure that's much better. But at least it wasn't an F-bomb."

"Say what's in your heart," Heather said.

"Grand idea," Fred agreed.

My sister was right. She was usually right. However, I needed someone else with us to do it correctly. I held up a finger to Gideon, who seemed a bit confused. Hustling over to June, I held out my arms for my baby. In order to marry Gideon, we needed our entire little family together. With our child cradled to my chest, I walked back to the man I wanted to spend my long life with. His smile was what I expected. The happy tears in his eyes, I did not. For a Demon, the guy was in touch with his emotions. He was a keeper.

He pulled us close and whispered in my ear. "Say your vows, Counselor."

"Getting there, Reaper," I replied as Alana Catherine reached up and pulled his hair with a giggle that made my waterworks turn on. I inhaled deeply and blew it out slowly. Speaking from my heart was easy. I was so filled with love I just let it rip. "Gideon, you're the love of my life—my best friend. I promise you this, every day, I will cherish you. I will love you. I will laugh and cry with you. I'll be by your side to kick some ass when necessary, which I hope we get a break from for a little while." The crowd laughed. They got it. We all needed a freaking break. "I'm your ride or die, and you're mine. I don't know what I did in my life to get so lucky, but I'm thankful for it with all of my heart. Together, we'll have a home full of love for our daughter, and I want to live each day of our seriously long lives with you by my side. I promise to be your partner, lover and bestie until the end of time. My life truly started the day I met you."

Gideon's grin set my thong on fire, and the kiss he planted on my lips made my head spin.

"Keep your tongue in your mouth, boy," Candy grunted, slapping the Grim Reaper on the back of the head. "You need to pull some vows out of your butt, and then I'll say the man and wife shit." She checked her notes on the toothpick box. "After that, you can go on up to your room and bang. Got it?"

"Got it," Gideon said with a wince and a chuckle. He turned his attention to me and got very serious. "Daisy, my life started when you came into it. You make it worth living and even though I didn't know it, I've been waiting an eternity for you. Literally." His lopsided grin made my knees weak. "It wasn't until you came into my life that I truly understood what love meant. You and Alana Catherine are the reasons for each and every breath I take." He paused and chuckled. "Kind of like the stalker song that was played when you walked down the aisle."

I laughed. Hard. The queens didn't. They were wildly confused.

"That being said," Gideon continued. "I promise to be your husband, best friend, lover and partner in juicy boner justice until the end of time." I giggled, and he grinned. "I promise to love, cherish and worship you and our daughter. I will protect you with my life… because my existence would be meaningless without you. I love you."

"Love you more," I whispered.

"Not possible," he shot back.

"You done, fucker?" Candy Vargo asked Gideon.

"For the love of everything, you ain't supposed to say at a wedding," Gram grumbled. "Candy Vargo, you're makin' my rump itch. I swear I'm gonna jerk you bald if you don't control that potty mouth."

"Will do, Gram," Candy said, blanching. Only Gram could put the Keeper of Fate in her place without being electrocuted. Gram might be dead, but she still ruled the roost.

"Yes, I'm done," Gideon said.

"Okay then, by the power vested in me because I took an online crash course in officiating weddings, I now pronounce you husband and wife. You can now stick your tongue down Daisy's throat or go on upstairs and bang. However, it is rather obvious you've had premarital sex due to the bundle of joy in your hands…" She waved a hand in front of her face and wrinkled her nose. "Who may or may not have just pooped her pants."

It wasn't a typical wedding, but we weren't typical. And Candy was correct. Alana Catherine had just dropped a few friends off at the lake. It would be dealt with shortly. But it could wait a minute. Now, it was time for a lip lock with my *husband.*

Gideon dipped his head, his warm lips brushing against mine. I melted into his arms, my fingers lacing behind his neck as I kissed him right back.

The deal was sealed, and nothing in the world could make me happier.

CHAPTER TWO

GIDEON AND I WERE COMMANDED TO TAKE A QUICK BREAK TO change clothes for the reception. The queens, with naughty expressions on their faces, insisted they needed an hour to set up the finale of the extravaganza. Heather and Missy took Alana Catherine for a diaper change and stroller ride. Candy Vargo mentioned the banging part of the vows again and only stopped pontificating about it when Gram threatened to cancel her birth certificate. Everyone else tried to hide their grins and pretend they had no clue what was going on.

They failed and were fooling no one.

We were fooling no one as we casually walked back into the house then raced up the stairs to our bedroom like horny teenagers.

"We've got an hour," Gideon said, tearing his tux off and tossing it aside. He made quick work of my gown before throwing me onto the bed. "Let's not waste a second of it."

"Deal," I said, as he fell onto the bed next to me. I climbed on top of him, straddling my man and smiling so hard my face hurt.

Stuff was about to get sweaty, sexy and good. We were both a hundred thousand percent committed. The odds were excellent for an orgasmic time.

~

"HOLY HELL," GIDEON SAID WITH AN EXHAUSTED LAUGH AS HE pulled me into a hug and kissed the top of my head.

My hair was no longer in a lovely upswept do. It was wild— as wild as the sex we'd had for the past hour. Our bed looked like a tornado had hit it, and I'd been kind of worried our friends and family might hear us. Whatever. I'd ceased to care about that after the first earthquake-inducing orgasm.

"This might sound insane, but I think married sex beats single sex." I traced his full lips with my finger.

"I'm inclined to agree," he said with the grin of a very satiated man. "But maybe we should go another round to make sure."

I rolled over and checked my watch. "Can't. We'll be late to our own reception. You think four times wasn't enough?"

He raised a brow and gave me a *look*. All he had to do was rake me over with his gorgeous eyes, and I was ready to go. Orgasms with my husband were beyond awesome. Like Lays Potato Chips… one, or four in my case, was never enough.

"A hundred times wouldn't be enough," he informed me in a voice so sexy, I considered taking him up on his offer.

"A hundred times in a row might kill us," I pointed out with a giggle.

"Not a problem. We're Immortal." His smile was positively feral.

I was soooo tempted, but we had an eternity to make love. And we would take full advantage of that lovely fact.

"Fine point. Well made," I said, reluctantly slipping out of his embrace and grabbing the dress the queens had provided for the reception. "However, we have an elegaaanza extravagaaaanza," I elongated the words, mimicking the queens for dramatic effect, "to go to, and I want to dance with my husband and daughter. Plus, I'm pretty sure if we're late, Candy Vargo will come up here and drag us to the party naked."

"There's a visual that just killed my libido," he said with a groan as he put his tux back on.

"I'm good like that," I told him, stepping into the amazing Prada wedges that went perfectly with the Marchesa gown the boys had chosen. While sequins weren't normally my thing, the gown was to die for—the intricate threadwork woven in with teal sequins and floral applique was delicate and exquisite. The dress shimmered when I moved. It felt alive and magical on my body. In my wedding gown, I'd felt like a princess. In my party dress, I felt like a freaking queen. Quickly twisting my hair back up, I reapplied the lipstick that had been kissed off and was ready to rumble.

"I have a stunning wife," Gideon said, admiring me.

"And I have a sexy badass husband," I told him.

He kissed me sweetly and cupped my chin in his hand. "You happy?"

I sighed happily. I finally had everything I'd ever dreamed of and more than I could've ever imagined. I had great friends who always had my back, sisters and brothers who I cherished, my gram, my child, and the most delicious, handsome hunk of a husband that I loved more than life itself.

Our eyes met, and I told him with all sincerity, "More than I've ever thought possible."

He smiled as he wrapped his arms around me and kissed

me again. The warmth of his embrace, and the tenderness in his lips as they moved against mine nearly brought me to tears. I'd never felt so beautiful or wanted.

"I plan to make your happiness my only mission for the rest of our lives," he whispered against my lips.

"You don't even have to try to succeed at that," I said, giving him a final kiss. As much as I was enjoying the moment, we had a lifetime of them coming, and our guests, who had taken time out of their lives to celebrate us, were waiting downstairs. "You ready to party with the crazies?"

"I am," he replied, picking me up as if I weighed no more than a feather before whisking me down the stairs to the party.

It was time to get to the reception before the reception came to us.

"LET THE FESTIVITIES BEGIN!" WALLY SHOUTED AS CARL CLAPPED his hands and produced a karaoke machine.

My hope for a party without a version of *Islands in the Stream* sung in the key of X by Carl and Dirk was dashed. But I didn't care. It wouldn't be an extravaganza without karaoke sung by some tone-deaf drag queens—at least that's what Wally had said.

Food and drink had been placed on long, elaborately decorated, flower-covered tables. Tim had cooked up a storm. There were hot dishes in all varieties—even vegetarian for me. It smelled rank, but he was so proud of himself that everyone partook. Mirror balls dropped from the tree branches and the queens had removed all the chairs from the ceremony and placed them at the large round tables that had magically appeared. A temporary dance floor had been centrally located, perfect for shaking your groove thing. The dead had already started, and parts were flying off them as they flapped their arms...or what was left of their arms in some of their cases.

I shook my head at the sight.

Watching three hundred ghosts do the Chicken Dance was something I'd never in my life thought I'd see. It got even weirder when Candy Vargo started clucking and pretending to lay an egg out of her butt. At least, she was having fun. She hadn't even noticed that about a hundred specters had flown away in horror.

Glittering pink and champagne-colored balloons floated in the air much to the delight of the jubilant guests—especially our baby. Alana Catherine squealed with joy every time one floated by her. I'd never been hugged and kissed so much in my life. I held my daughter in my arms, and my *husband* stood at our side. It was every kind of wonderful.

Until it wasn't...

"What the fuck is that?" Candy Vargo shouted, pointing to the sky.

Three blindingly bright lights were headed our way. They bounced through the air clumsily and crashed into each other multiple times.

"Aliens?" Carl squawked.

"I think UFOs," Dirk squealed.

Tim immediately pulled out his notebook. He glanced up at the incoming lights then spoke. "Doesn't look like any UFO I've seen," he said. "But a total of 12,618 sightings have been recorded from 1948 until 1969. I'm quite sure the recent numbers are much higher."

"How in the fuck is that helping?" Candy demanded, tossing her toothpicks in the air, then waving her hands and arming herself like she was ready to go into battle.

"I don't know," Tim said frantically. "My go-to instinct in times of danger is reciting facts. And speaking of... did you know that thousands of Americans have taken out insurance against aliens?"

Heather rolled her eyes, her multitude of tattoos doing a war dance along her skin as she prepared for the incoming fight. "Not helping. Everyone, get in a line. If we have to, we'll destroy it. However, we need to figure out if they come in peace before we blow them up."

No, no, no, I thought. *Not on my freaking wedding day!* I'd be damned if some extraterrestrial from outer space was going to ruin my special day.

"Excellent thinking," Charlie said as his eyes went icy blue and his badass showed. "Rafe, Prue and Abby, get June, Amelia, Missy, Jennifer and Alana Catherine into the house. Gideon, drop a ward around it once they're inside."

Things were getting serious. *Shit, shit, shit.*

"On it," Gideon said, ushering the humans and our child to safety.

The lights were still zig-zagging toward us, getting bigger by the second. "Ghosts," I shouted, my hands sparking like they were about to detonate. "I want you to hide. We don't know the intentions of the umm... aliens... or, whatever they are. Until we do, disappear. NOW."

In a gust of wind, the dead vanished from sight. I shook my head. Was I ever going to get a day of freaking peace? It certainly didn't seem like it.

"Ward has been dropped," Gideon said as he joined the line of defense.

I glanced over at him. "This is either going to turn out to be a great story or a shitshow. Thoughts?"

"I'm going with great story until further notice," he replied, watching the incoming lights warily. "However, if it becomes a shitshow, I'm ready."

I nodded and adjusted my expectations. "Me too."

And then something amazing happened.

Something unbelievable.

Something I didn't think was possible.

However, nothing was impossible... one just had to believe.

I squinted as the dots of light grew closer. From a distance, they had looked like balls of fire. At closer inspection... they didn't look like balls at all.

They were shaped like bodies. A surge of joy jolted through me when I recognized our incoming aliens as the ghostly bodies of three old women wearing conservative Chanel suits and sensible pumps.

"Well, I have fuckin' never," Candy Vargo shouted, tossing her sword to the ground and running toward the incoming *aliens*.

Tim joined her waving like a madman as the gals came in for a crash landing.

"Am I seeing what I think I'm seeing?" Heather asked with a laugh. Her magical tattoos were no longer dancing menacingly over her skin. Instead, they were waltzing blissfully up and down her arms.

"Umm... yes," I said, already crying. "Gideon, drop the ward. Tell everyone to come back out. We have some late guests."

Lura Belle, Jolly Sue and Dimple were definitely dead, but they looked pretty darn good for getting torn apart and sucked into a vortex of deadly Purgatory magic.

"Hello, all you fly-bitten moldwarps," Lura Belle said with a silly smile on her normally pursed cat-butt lips. "What did we miss while we were indisposed?"

17

"A fuckin' wedding," Candy said.

"Unacceptable," Jolly Sue grumbled. "We've only been gone a few days, and you boil-brained, goatish canker-blossoms had a wedding without us?"

"Oh my," Dimple fretted. "It's a very haggard, fat-kidneyed hugger-mugger thing to not include us!"

I agreed. I walked over to the Nephilim and hugged each one of them. Parts of their bodies went right through mine. Still, I was able to feel them, and they could feel me. "Welcome back. Can you stay a while?"

"I have no clue," Dimple admitted. "However, we're here now. I insist the wedding be redone. It's rude not to."

I turned and looked at Gideon. He simply shrugged. "I'd marry you a thousand times over. I'm in."

"Candy? Can you pull that crap you said out of your butt again?" I asked.

"I just pulled an imaginary chicken egg out of my ass," she reminded me. "Of course, I can yank a few F-bombs out and remarry you fuckers."

I snorted. It was unavoidable. "Alrighty then. Let's get married."

"Hang on," Lura Belle said, looking up at the sky and growing increasingly uncomfortable. "We have a message."

"From who?" I asked, feeling a little wonky but unsure why.

"The Higher Power," she said.

Now I knew why I felt wonky. Not much good came via the Higher Power.

"The message?" I held my breath, waiting for the answer.

"They're coming back," Lura Belle relayed. "The balance has shifted and must be repaired. If not… it will be a problem."

I had so many questions, but I would deal with one at a time. "Who is coming back?"

"I don't know," Lura Belle admitted.

"Can you define *problem?*" I pressed, knowing it was probably futile.

Again, she didn't know.

We all stood in silence and mulled over the new wrinkle that could unravel our lives... again. Catching a break and going on vacation was looking less likely.

"Holy motherfuckin' shitballs," Candy Vargo shouted. "What the actual fuck?"

I whipped around in the direction of Candy's voice and gasped. What the actual fuck was correct.

On my front porch, transparent shoulder to transparent shoulder, stood some very familiar people to me. My gut clenched and my skin turned clammy. The group was expressionless and appeared scared.

Slowly, I walked toward the porch. Gideon fell in step to my right. Charlie to my left. Candy Vargo, Tim, Tory and Heather backed up Charlie. Gabe, Rafe, Prue and Abby stayed on Gideon's side. Zander and Catriona were behind me and the Four Horsemen of the Apocalypse brought up the rear.

I wasn't terrified of what I saw, but I was worried... worried for the ones on my porch. Something had gone wrong, terribly wrong.

"Steve?" I called out.

My dead husband barely acknowledged me. It was as if he couldn't understand. He trembled and faded in and out. Standing beside him was Sam, Sister Catherine, Agnes, Birdie and John. They weren't supposed to be here. They'd gone into the Light. I'd seen them go into the Light. I'd helped them do it.

But they were back.

Agnes floated forward. She was a shell of who she'd been. The joy and vitality had been stripped from her. Her vocal rhythm was staccato and off. Her words were even worse. "Fix the rift in the chain, Angel of Mercy. If unattended, evil from the Darkness will descend on the earth and tear it open for good. Death and destruction will rule."

"How?" I asked, hoping for more… a clue, a hint. I didn't even care if it was cryptic. Hell, I'd do the Chicken Dance and shit out eggs for a cryptic clue right now.

The dead on my porch said nothing. They just stared at me. It was unnerving.

As they began to fade away, Steve stepped forward. For a brief moment, he was back to the wonderful man who I'd spent so many years with. "Daisy," he whispered brokenly. "You have only days to discover the riddle and solve it. Start with the ending you desire and work your way back. It's the only way. Remember nothing is impossible… you just have to believe."

As he shimmered and grew fainter, I spoke up. "Will you be back?"

He smiled. It was filled with sadness. "I will. Though, I'm not really sure why I'm here. Work fast, Daisy. The Light depends on you."

In a gust of icy wind, the dead on my porch disappeared. I turned and looked at Gideon. His expression was unreadable as he stared back at me. My stress felt as if it was eating me alive. Peeling off my skin wouldn't even bother me right now.

"Suggestions?" I asked the Immortals who I trusted with my life.

All I got in response was silence until Lura Belle spoke. "Call me crazy, but I'd start with the Higher Power."

I closed my eyes and wanted to be somewhere else— anywhere else. The best day of my life had taken a seriously messed up turn.

"Bad fuckin' idea," Candy Vargo grunted.

"I'd have to agree," Charlie said tightly.

"You have a better one?" I asked, feeling like I was having an out-of-body experience and watching the scene unfold below.

No one did.

"I'm putting on sweats and tennis shoes," I announced as I marched up the steps to the porch.

"Because?" Heather asked warily.

"Because my dress is fabulous, and I'm not going to mess it up when I kick the Higher Power's ass."

"Ohhhhh shit," Candy Vargo muttered.

I stopped at the front door, turned around and faced my family and friends. "Who's with me?"

Gideon stepped forward immediately, followed by the queens and Candy Vargo. Without hesitation, Heather and my other siblings, along with Tory, Charlie, Tim, Zander and Catriona joined the crew.

"What exactly are we going to fuckin' do?" Candy asked, handing me a toothpick.

I popped it in my mouth and leveled her with a hard gaze. "I have no idea," I admitted. "But I will tell you this, the Higher Power is gonna rue the day it messed with my wedded bliss."

My voice sounded sure and strong. The truth was that I was anything but sure and strong. However, I was going to fake it until I made it. It had worked so far. The Higher Power was in for a surprise. A pissed-off bride who happened to be the Angel of Mercy was about to fuck up Its day, the way It had fucked up mine.

I just hoped I would live to the last chapter of my next adventure in one piece. Midlife had turned out to be a ride, both good and bad. I was leaner and meaner due to my job.

However, I was still me, and I had plans to live in peace, not pieces.

Anything was possible if I believed. I believed. The Higher Power was about to get a lesson in real faith. If the Higher Power thought it was fun to play life and death games with me, It would lose.

All I wanted was to have the time of my midlife, and that was still my plan. Even if it took me until my last breath to get there.

CHAPTER THREE

THE GREAT ROOM IN OUR HOME WAS HUGE. HOWEVER, IT FELT cramped and tiny at the moment. A few of the champagne-colored balloons floated around, reminding me that it was my wedding day. However, it felt like it had occurred weeks ago. The mood was no longer festive. Not only were all the living and breathing people who attended my wedding present but over three hundred ghosts as well. With all the agitated dead chattering and wailing, I couldn't think straight. The big screen TV, at full volume, was on the game show channel and a rerun of *The Price Is Right* with Bob Barker joyously describing the final showcase. While fifty or so of the ghosts were glued to the screen, yelling prices for a boat, golf clubs, and a year's supply of ham, the rest were zipping around the room in distress, losing arms and legs all over the place. I was pretty sure there was a head rolling around on the floor but decided not to look too closely. Everything could be superglued back on eventually—stress on the word *eventually*. There was no time for specter surgery right now. Tim quietly offered bowls filled with unidentifiable substances for our guests to snack on. The thought was lovely. The aroma was not. The only beings excited to eat Tim's offerings were my dogs, Donna and Karen. That would end with some gnarly canine gas, but I had bigger problems.

Dirk, Wally, Carl and Fred, aka the Four Horsemen of the Apocalypse, had called to their horses and saddled up in the kitchen. Candy Vargo let them know in no uncertain terms if the steeds crapped in the house, she would make the queens eat it. Knowing Candy Vargo made good on her threats, they quickly galloped their steeds through the great room and into the yard, taking the front door with them. Candy had instructed them to be on the lookout for anything unusual, but all things considered, unusual had a broad definition for four drag queens sporting sequins, fangs and horns while riding around on huge horses.

Shoving my hands into the pockets of my army-green combat pants so I didn't accidentally or on purpose electrocute anyone was prudent. The thoughts racing in my mind literally made me dizzy. Taking out my unhinged frustrations on innocent ghosts—no matter how out of control— was a no-no.

The only ghosts not present were the ones who weren't supposed to be here. Where they'd gone, I had no clue. However, finding them was on the list. Seeing Steve again was unsettling. In a perfect world, my dead husband would have been a guest at my wedding to Gideon. He'd been so happy I'd found someone to love me the way I deserved to be loved. The world was far from perfect. Pinching myself to make sure I was awake, a new bruise on my thigh confirmed that I hadn't dreamed up what we'd all seen. Luck didn't seem to be on my side today.

Gideon placed a hand on my shoulder. In my husband's other arm was our daughter. Shockingly, she was sound asleep.

The sight of the two people I loved most in the world quieted a small part of the crazy in my brain. His steady gaze met my wild one. His touch calmed me, but I still felt the need to jump out of my skin.

"Send the ghosts away," he said. "There's a glitch and I'm not sure the dead are safe right now."

"In general, or around me?" I questioned.

He shrugged and shook his head. Well, crap. If the Grim Reaper didn't have the answer, no one did.

The bottom line was that he was correct about there being a glitch. It was the most rational explanation for the seriously irrational appearance of ghosts who should've completed their journeys to the other side. Inhaling deeply, I steeled my courage as I lightly touched Alana Catherine's precious head to center myself. Freaking out would help no one.

Tamping down the need to scream or do property damage, I cleared my throat, turned off the TV, and glanced up at my transparent guests, who were flying willy-nilly all over the place. "Okay. Listen up," I announced in my outdoor voice.

There needed to be less people in my home. Too many cooks were going to end up creating something horrendous. Kind of like one of Tim's casseroles but deadly.

I didn't think. I went with my gut. "Here's the deal. I want the ghosts to go to my old farmhouse for safety. Dead friends, please find and pick up your unattached appendages and keep them with you. If you're not sure where they are or if they belong to you, just grab whatever arm, leg or head you see and take them with you. We'll figure out who they match with later. I promise I'll glue you all back together as soon as I solve the... umm... issue."

I closed my eyes for a hot sec and swallowed the desire to laugh hysterically at the words that had just left my mouth.

Everything was sideways and wrong. However, it was my life, and there was no one else stepping up to live it.

"Rafe, Prue, Abby and Gabe, will you take the dead to the farmhouse and protect them, please?"

My siblings nodded immediately.

Tory stepped forward. "If the ghosts are in peril I'll go as well. As a last resort, I can take them to Purgatory. No one, even the Higher Power, can harm them there."

My stomach cramped. That wasn't in the plan at all. "Can they come back from Purgatory? Can they come home to me?"

Her pause was too long for my liking. "Most likely, yes."

I squinted at her. My voice was flat and sounded harsher than I'd intended. "*Most likely* doesn't work."

If my three hundred-ish deceased house guests—including Gram, Mr. Jackson, Lura Belle, Jolly Sue and Dimple—got stuck in Purgatory until Judgement Day I'd lose my shit.

Shaking my head, I stared at Tory. She was my friend, and I trusted her, but her *last resort* plan was a bad one. I was responsible for the ghosts. Purgatory might be safe, but it was not a good place to be. Getting stuck there was out of the question. "That's a hard no. Keep the dead in the farmhouse. Rafe, drop a protection ward. Let no one in or out unless Gideon or I give the go ahead."

"As you wish, Daisy," he said. "I'd like Amelia to be with me."

"Of course," I replied. And then to my surprise, Prue spoke up.

"I think for defensive purposes..." She looked extremely uncomfortable as she rocked back and forth on her feet. "Zander and Catriona might be... you know... umm... helpful."

My brows shot up. I was pretty sure if they could have, they would have met my hairline. Prue's request wasn't unreasonable as far as defense went, but there was far more to it. I stole a quick glance at Zander. He was as surprised as I was, but the man was also delighted. He had it bad for my sister, and she'd been studiously ignoring him.

While I was dying to ask questions, I didn't. Embarrassing her wasn't on the agenda. My siblings finding happiness after thousands of years of misery was at the top of my wish list after getting the ghosts back where they belong and living happily ever after with my man. Gabe and Tory were beginning to work on their happily ever after. Amelia and Rafe were already on their way. If Prue and Zander were meant to be, they would have my blessing. That left Abby, but since we lived forever—hopefully—she still had time to meet her other half.

"It's a solid fuckin' plan," Candy Vargo said. "I'd suggest sending Missy, June and Jennifer with them."

"I might look delicate," June said with a wink and a smile. "However, I'm made of steel like the claw end of a hammer."

I smiled back. No one was sure if June was Immortal or not. I'd saved my dear friend's life when I'd returned her soul to her body after the former Angel of Mercy, Clarissa, had stolen it. I'd told Charlie to envision June in his mind to help me out. He did. However, he'd envisioned his wife as the young woman he'd met decades before. So, when she'd come back to life, my magic had turned her back into the woman she'd been in her twenties instead of her fifties. In my defense, I'd had no idea if reviving June was even going to be possible, let alone that it would turn her young.

Initially, the transformation had been a bit of a shitshow since they had grown kids, but a little magic from Tim helped her look her real age for short periods of time. Charlie, as an Immortal, could choose his age. When June looked young, so did he. When they visited their kids and grandkids, he appeared to be in his sixties. In reality, he was a bazillion years old. The fact that the majority of my friends, including Gideon, were older than dirt was something I didn't know if I'd ever wrap my mind around.

Maybe when I was five hundred I'd get it. However, I was forty. Getting it wasn't gonna happen today.

Glancing over at Candy Vargo, I waited to hear what she had to say. She might be horribly dressed and profane as all get out, but she was normally the voice of reason. As the Keeper of Fate, I'd put my trust in her many times and would continue to do so. I was also surprised that she hadn't included my baby in the list of people to leave.

"Thoughts?" I asked her.

Candy removed the toothpick from her mouth and tossed it over her shoulder. Manners were something else the woman was lacking. "Lemme think," she muttered as she walked over to the coffee table, opened up a fresh box of toothpicks and scattered them on the table.

Slowly, she lined them up next to each other. Candy Vargo was meticulous and precise. Each of the pieces of wood was placed in a row evenly. There had to be about fifty. When she was done, she pointed at Jennifer, June and Missy. "Get your asses over here."

The three women walked over to the table. Heather was right behind Missy. Charlie followed June. That made sense. They were their partners in this life. Jennifer walked alone. She had a guy, but he was human. Sherriff Dip Doody was the man she refused to marry because she loved him too much to screw it up with a piece of paper. It made perfect sense since my Botox loving buddy had been married and divorced multiple times. While Jennifer knew about the secret world that existed right under the noses of the humans, Dip did not, and it had to stay that way. It had been shocking to witness how unafraid Jennifer was when she realized most of her friend group wasn't exactly human. Her only disappointment was that we didn't sparkle like the vampires in *Twilight*. My dear friend was one of a kind and the mold had been broken the day she was born.

Jennifer wasn't alone for long. Her BFF Tim hustled over and had her back. I had no clue what Candy Vargo was up to, but I waited impatiently for her to reveal her plan. Gideon stood beside me with Alana Catherine still asleep in his arms. He was alert and focused on whatever was about to happen. With the Keeper of Fate running the show, one never knew.

"Alrighty, fuckers," Candy Vargo announced.

"Language," Gram shouted as she darted over and waved a transparent finger in Candy's face. "You watch that mouth, girlie. You're makin' my rump itch. I love you like a daughter, but I'm gonna jerk you bald if you keep callin' your friends duckers."

"I said fuckers not duckers," Candy Vargo corrected Gram.

"Lord, have mercy," Gram said, smacking Candy in the back of the head. Her hand went right through, but the intent was clear. Candy blanched. Yes, Gram was dead, but she still ruled the roost and definitely ruled Candy Vargo. Love did things like that, and Gram loved Candy. "I know what you said. I ain't gonna repeat it. I want you to try again and not call your friends nasty names."

Candy Vargo was wildly confused. She used the F-bomb as a verb, noun, adverb, adjective, preposition, conjunction and interjection. In the midst of the chaos we were living, I almost laughed.

"Assholes?" Candy tried.

"Heck to the no," Gram snapped.

"Dicks?" Candy asked, clearly thinking that dicks would pass muster.

Gram just gave her the evil eye.

The Keeper of Fate ran her hand over her face as she tried to come up with an endearment that wasn't disgusting. She was having a tremendously difficult time. The ghosts were loving the Candy show almost as much as *The Price is Right*.

"Wankers?" Candy suggested.

Gram shook her head as the deceased audience laughed uproariously. When the dead laughed, to say it was alarming was an understatement. The sound reminded me of a prolonged and booming death rattle. It had taken some getting used to. Now, the off-putting sound made me smile. Happy came in many sizes and sounds in my life.

Candy Vargo glanced around. "Can one of you shitbags help a girl out?" she demanded.

I blew out a long breath and shook my head. She was never gonna get it. "Use names. It's your safest bet."

She flipped me the bird which doubled as a thumbs up in Candy's world. "Got it. Alright, June, Jennifer and Missy. Each of you are gonna pick a stick."

"Wait," I said. "Is this random or do you know what you're doing?"

Candy Vargo rolled her eyes so hard I could only see the whites of her eyes. "Do I look fuckin' random to you, jackass?"

There were so many ways to answer. I decided to play it safe. Getting my house blown up was something I wasn't up for. "No."

"That's right," she grunted. "Everybody—meaning Daisy—needs to keep their cake holes shut or I'm gonna shut it for you."

I nodded and flipped her off. She seemed satisfied.

"At the risk of having my cake hole removed, I have a question," Jennifer said.

Again, with the eye roll from Candy. "What?"

"When do we pick the stick?"

"Good question," Candy Vargo said as Jennifer blew out a loud and relieved sigh. It was clear that she was pleased she was going to keep her cake hole. "The answer is after I do a little thingie."

Pressing my lips together so hard it hurt, I stopped myself from asking her to define 'thingie.' None of this sounded good to me.

The Keeper of Fate began to glow bright orange as she waved her hands over the toothpicks. She chanted in a language that I didn't understand. It was melodic and guttural at the same time. A shimmering lime-green mist formed a small funnel over the table and hovered over the toothpicks. When Candy clapped her hands, the mist dissolved into crystals of the same lime green and covered the table. The toothpicks were now glowing brighter than Candy Vargo. "Now you pick a pick," she announced.

One by one, Jennifer, Missy and June chose a toothpick and held it up. Candy swiped her hand over the table and scattered the rest of the toothpicks. The minute she did it, they lost their glow. The ones held by my friends still shone brightly.

The Keeper of Fate examined Missy's toothpick first. She stared at it for several minutes. "Missy, you and Heather will go to Heather's place. Stay by your fuckin' cell phones and be ready to transport if I call. Missy, you're gonna need to be prepared to take souls into your body."

Missy paled a bit, then nodded. My best friend since I was a child was a Soul Keeper. Unknowingly, Missy had kept my mother and Birdie safe for decades. Her gift was rare and powerful. I'd be grateful until the end of time that she'd protected my mother.

"How many?" Missy asked.

Candy shrugged. "Don't know. How many you got room for?"

It was Missy's turn to shrug. "Not a clue."

Candy Vargo picked up a few toothpicks off the floor and put them into her mouth. "Welp, hopefully, we're not gonna have to find that out. Heather, drop a ward around your house. Don't let nobody in there."

"Will do," my sister said, taking Missy's hand in hers. She turned to me and reached her other hand out. I took it. "You've got this, Daisy."

"I do," I said with more confidence than I felt.

With a quick squeeze and a kiss to my cheek, Heather and Missy transported away in an icy blue mist.

Candy moved to June next and examined her toothpick. "June, you're goin' to the farmhouse with the others."

"Well, shoot," June said with a sigh. "I was hoping to be able to help."

Candy Vargo leaned in and hugged June. She liked June. Hell, everybody liked June. She was one of the kindest people I knew. "You will be helpin'. All them ghosts need a steady presence like you. The rest of them going over there except Amelia are batshit."

"We can hear you," Gabe pointed out.

Candy cackled. "Yep, I know."

"And on that lovely note," Abby said with a raised brow and a naughty smirk. "I say we leave before this chat degenerates into name calling, which would lead to violence and might even end with... a little cannibalism."

"FOR FUCKS SAKE," Candy Vargo bellowed. "I eat people one fuckin' time, and no one can let it go."

I winced and closed my eyes. The relationship between Candy and my Angel siblings was iffy at best. Gabe, Prue, Abby and Rafe had been eaten by Candy centuries ago. Granted, they'd tried to destroy her on Zadkiel's dastardly orders, and she'd apparently done what she had to do being legless and armless. To this day, I couldn't comprehend how my two sisters and two brothers were actually alive. The logistics were mind-boggling and stomach-churning. Part of me wanted the particulars, but my sense of self-preservation and my aversion to puking stopped me. Some things were better left unexplained.

"Shall we?" Rafe said, glancing up at the ghosts.

The garbled replies were affirmative. In less time than it took to blink, Gabe, Rafe, Abby, Prue, Tory, Amelia, Zander, Catriona and June, along with the gaggle of ghosts, disappeared.

The great room was far less crowded. However, not all the ghosts had left. The three of them remaining made sense. Dimple, Jolly Sue and Lura Belle had come back to give me the message. Having them here was smart. However, there were two that I wanted gone. I knew we needed to hear the verdict on Jennifer's toothpick, but I had some business to deal with first.

"Gram, you and Mr. Jackson need to leave."

"Daisy girl, I ain't goin' nowhere," Gram informed me in the voice she used when I was a teenager and wanted to move my curfew out much later than the one she'd given me.

I hadn't won then, but I would win now.

"You're going," I corrected her.

She raised a ghostly brow and crossed her skinny arms

33

over her chest. "I was the Death Counselor before you, and I know a thing or two about it."

I shook my head. "Gram, I want you safe. I don't know what's happening."

"But you're willin' to put yourself at risk to figure it out?" she challenged.

I sighed and ran my hands through my hair. "That's kind of my job."

"And you're my job, little missy," she shot back.

Gram was a force to be reckoned with, but I was up for the reckoning. "I can't lose you. That terrifies me."

She smiled and cupped my cheek with her cool, papery hand. "Oh darlin', shared joy means twice the joy. Shared fear means half the fear. Ain't no man or woman is an island. As my foul-mouthed chosen daughter says, don't fuck with fate. If you're given a gift, take it and say thank you. I'm your gift, baby girl."

I almost swallowed my tongue. Gram did not use the F-bomb. Ever. The old gal wasn't playing.

"I think I said don't fuckin' fuck with fate," Candy Vargo volunteered.

Gram groaned. "You did. I was tryin' to make it a little less offensive."

"My bad," Candy muttered with a grin.

"I should say so," Gram retorted. "And wipe that there grin off your face, or I'm gonna tie your knickers in a knot, Candy Vargo. That's the only dang time you're gonna hear the F-bomb from my mouth."

"Yes, ma'am," Candy replied, covering her mouth with her hand to hide the grin that was impossible to hide.

I wasn't going to win this fight. Every day, I learned that things in our Immortal world rarely happened without reason. If Gram was certain she needed to stay, she needed to stay.

"You win, old lady… and thank you," I said, smiling at her. "But I think Mr. Jackson should leave."

"No can do," Gram told me. "Mr. Jackson is my beau. We're courtin' now. Where he goes, I go. And where I go, he goes. We're both old and dead. We don't know how much time we have left. My man is as fine as a frog hair split four ways and I don't want any of them other lady ghosts tryin' to steal him away."

Mr. Jackson laughed and wrapped his good arm around Gram. "Nooooooah channnceah ooooof thaaata! Haaappyah asssssss a poossummah eaaaatin sweeeeetah poooootaaaatoes!"

"What the hell did he just say?" Candy asked, squinting at the ghost.

Gram giggled like a school girl. "Mr. Jackson said he's as happy with me as a possum eatin' sweet potatoes! That right there just dills my pickles."

They kissed, and their heads went right through each other's.

All of this was news to me. My dead grandmother had a dead boyfriend who was missing half of his noggin. Literally. Granted, I adored the old man. He was sweet as could be. If Gram was happy, I was happy for her.

I began to pace the room. The living people left were Gideon, Alana Catherine, Charlie, Candy Vargo, Tim, Jennifer, the four queens outside atop their steeds and me. It was time to get back to the toothpick. Candy was already on it.

"Well, knock me over with a fuckin' feather," she muttered, staring at the small piece of wood Jennifer held up for observation. "I'm a little confused."

"Define confused," I said, stopping in front of her.

"Welp," Candy said, scratching her head. "It's the kind of confused where I'm not real sure if I could find my ass right now even if I stuck my hands in my underpants."

"I didn't think you wore underpants," Tim said.

Gram groaned. Dimple, Lura Belle and Jolly Sue just tssked and fanned their wildly offended selves with their hands. The rest of us... we were used to it. Candy Vargo was so wrong she was right. Underpants or not, she was a badass.

"I don't wear grundies," Candy Vargo confirmed, pulling up the back of her dress and mooning us. "I'm just tryin' to explain how confused I am without saying fuck a bunch of times. I know exactly where my ass is since I slap it on the regular. I just thought the analogy was good."

"Makes sense," Tim told her, reaching over and pulling her dress back down.

Looking at the Keeper of Fates butt wasn't on my bingo card for today, or ever. Knowing that she slapped it on the regular was something I would need therapy to forget. "Explain what you saw," I instructed, hoping to avoid any more talk about Candy Vargo's privates.

Candy examined Jennifer's toothpick one last time and sighed. "She's supposed to stay right here."

That didn't make any sense. But nothing made all that much sense right now.

"I'm fine with that," Jennifer said, pulling a bottle of wine out of her bag and uncorking it. "Do you think the Higher Power might sparkle like Edward?"

"Who is Edward?" Charlie asked.

"That cutie vampire from *Twilight*," she replied, pouring herself a glass of white.

"Umm... doubtful," I told her. Or maybe not. What did I

know? Nothing. I knew nothing at the moment. However, there were other things to be discussed.

"What about Alana Catherine?" Gideon asked the question that was about to come out of my mouth. "Her safety is paramount."

Candy and Charlie walked over to the little gal in question. Charlie's eyes had gone a strange silver, and his power was evident. The air always grew as thick as molasses when Charlie went warrior on us.

"Tamp that shit back," Candy said, punching him in the arm. "Most of us like to breathe, jackass."

Charlie smiled. "Will do." He gently touched Alana Catherine's head. "I believe that decision should be made after we have a chat with a few others."

"Cryptic isn't gonna work," I told Charlie. I was over the Immortals speaking in vague hints.

His eyes still glowed, but the expression on his face was kind. "I quite agree, Daisy. I think we should bring in the Bitch Goddess Cecily. She just met with the Higher Power. The Goddess of the Darkness might have information that would be useful to us."

"Fuck. Fuckity, fuck, fuck, fuck," Candy muttered, walking over to the fireplace, waving her hands and starting a roaring fire.

I looked at Gideon. He stared back at me. Well, I supposed a fire in the correct place was better than Candy blowing the back wall off the house.

"Speak," I insisted. "Now."

She turned around. Her expression was hard and she was glowing. With the fire in back of her, she looked terrifying. "Cecily did indeed see the Higher Power. She got Pandora out of her, and now there are two Goddesses of the Darkness again."

"That's good, right?" I questioned. "The balance is in check."

"That part is good," Candy agreed in a tight tone. "However, Cecily threatened the Higher Power, and It's after her now."

"Wait. What?" Gideon ground out between clenched teeth, handing Alana Catherine over to me. "Why did we not know this?"

"No one asked," Candy pointed out. "It ain't our problem."

I handed my baby to Charlie. The Keeper of Fate might not have blown the back wall off the house, but I was tempted to. "It is now," I snapped. "You should have led with that."

Candy looked at the floor for a long beat. I wasn't sure if I was about to get electrocuted or not. I didn't care. Beating around the bush at this point was bullshit. There was some kind of tear in the Light and people who should be there had come back as shells of themselves. All of it was my problem.

I wasn't sure how great it was to owe a favor to the Goddess of the Darkness, but Cecily was now my niece by marriage and as new to this crazy as I was. Besides, I liked her and she liked me.

I turned to Gideon. "Call her. Ask her to come."

He nodded and pulled out his phone. As I'd heard the newly minted goddess say a few times… it was time to get the party started.

CHAPTER FOUR

"THEY'LL BE HERE SHORTLY," GIDEON SAID AS HE TOOK ALANA Catherine back from Charlie.

"They?" I asked.

"Cecily and Abaddon," he replied, sniffing our baby's bottom and wincing. "She pooped."

"I got it," Jennifer said, scooping a giggling Alana Catherine out of Gideon's arms and kissing her nose. "You guys can keep discussing all your sparkly friends. We'll be right back!"

My baby giggled all the way up the stairs as Jennifer sang a song about how everybody poops. I giggled, too. My dogs were right on Jennifer's heels, with their tails wagging a mile a minute. When she got to the part about how when *Candy Vargo poops her pants, they fall on the floor because she doesn't wear underpants*, even the Keeper of Fate threw back her head and laughed.

It was the little things I was living for right now. Laughing about poop might be on the humor level of a second-grade boy, but I'd take it. My daughter's giggle was the most gorgeous sound in the Universe. I was made whole by my child's laugh.

"I'd suggest we go over the discussion we had at Cecily's home in California before she visited the Higher Power," Tim announced, pulling out a notebook and pen from the pocket of his mail uniform. "There was much valuable information shared. Our situation is different, but knowledge is power."

Tim was correct. Before Cecily had embarked on that journey, Gideon, Candy Vargo, Charlie, Tim, Heather and I went to meet with her. I wasn't very useful, but my friends and family had been. Heather wasn't here now, but between the rest of us, we could piece it together. It would save time in the long run. If I was going to deal with the Higher Power, it was beneficial to know as much as possible.

"Darlings!" Dirk said, popping his head in where the front door used to be. "We've spotted nothing unusual yet! How's it going in here? Have the ones who should be in the Light come back?"

"No, not yet," I told him, glancing around just in case I was wrong. Honestly, I didn't know if we would see them again at all. Steve's words were forefront in my mind—'You have only days to discover the riddle and solve it. Start with the ending you desire and work your way back. It's the only way. Remember, nothing is impossible… you just have to believe.'

"Alrightyroo! Back to work!" Dirk blew kisses and returned to his post in the yard with the other queens.

I did believe, and I would continue to believe. But believing blindly wasn't something I was going to do. Getting armed with as much info as possible was my plan. "Should we just talk through what we recall?" I asked.

"How about we watch it?" Charlie suggested.

I looked at him warily. If he was suggesting we go back in

time and relive it, I was going to let him have it. Yep, he was the Immortal Enforcer and could end me with a blink of his eyes, but I was never turning time back again. I'd done it once and almost hadn't lived to tell. "And how exactly would we do that?"

Charlie chuckled. He'd clearly read my mind or, more likely, my expression. "On the big screen TV."

"Are you messing with me?" I asked, still cautious.

"Not at all, Daisy," he assured me as he approached the TV and snapped his fingers.

"I just love it when Charlie gives us a show." Tim clasped his hands together. "He so rarely does!"

"That's because giving the past the BlockBuster Video treatment takes a fuckload of magic, and the fucker is useless for a few hours afterward," Candy Vargo reminded Tim.

"Be kind and rewind a minute," I said to Charlie, taking the BlockBuster metaphor and running with it. "I don't want you to harm yourself. I might need you."

The Enforcer glanced over his shoulder and gave me a kind, fatherly smile. "Daisy, this journey isn't mine to make, but if you need me, the power drain won't last long. I'll be right as rain and back to full power in an hour or two. Besides, this is the clearest and most concise way to get the information you need. Watching what happened when Cecily came up against the Higher Power will be far more productive than trying to piece it together from a game of telephone with our memories. A lot has happened since the meeting, and perception colors the past."

A lot was an understatement. The Enforcer was offering a gift of clarity, and I was going to accept. "Thank you, Charlie. Please show us."

The images on the television were snowy for a moment,

but Charlie twirled his fingers, moved his arms like he was signaling a jet to land, and then clapped his hands. Immediately, the picture became crystal clear with Candy Vargo's mug front and center.

I stared at the television screen as the recent past came to life like an episode of *Big Brother*.

"Thank fucking God for that," on-screen Candy grunted, while standing in the middle of what I recognized as Cecily's bungalow living room in Venice, California.

On-screen Gideon, Tim, Charlie, and Heather, along with myself, were in the Dark Goddess's living room along with Cecily's mom, Lilith, and Cecily's agent, an Angel named Cher.

"Fascinating," Tim said, standing behind the couch, ready to take notes. "Charlie, you really are a marvel."

"Mind-blowing," I agreed.

The Immortal Enforcer's shoulders lifted and back straightened at the compliment.

"Anyone got popcorn?" Lura Belle asked, as she and her sisters sat on the loveseat to watch the show.

Gram and Mr. Jackson floated in the air near Charlie's head, and Gideon stood by me next to the couch. Jennifer hadn't yet returned with Alana Catherine, but the baby Death Counselor's poops could be almost supernaturally toxic, so I assumed she was going through a box of booty wipes.

Leaning forward, I focused on the TV screen.

"I look hot up on that fuckin' TV," Candy said. "Right?"

There was only one answer to that question that wouldn't end in bloodshed. "Very hot," I agreed. "Now, be quiet and watch."

"Speaking of," Cecily said, turning to the assembled group in her home. *"Explain to me how the Higher Power isn't God."*

Neither Cecily nor I were well-versed with the Bible. I

remembered being glad she asked the question instead of me. I'd taken far too much crap for not having read the book yet. I half expected someone to make a comment about it right now, but when I glanced around, everyone was glued to the screen.

In this episode of *This Is My Crazy Midlife*, Tim entered Cecily's cozy living room with one of his casseroles. The Dark Goddess's eyes grew huge when she caught a whiff, but she had better manners than me and didn't gag.

In the next scene, everyone was seated, except Gideon and Lilith weren't there. This was when Gideon, who was Lilith's brother, had taken the ex-goddess out of the room for a mental health break after Lilith had revealed some past unsavory behavior that had been relevant to Pandora's path to evil. Her actions hadn't necessarily been the cause of Pandora turning wicked, but it had definitely been a gateway. The revelation had been a shocker, especially for Cecily.

The rest of us watched with a small amount of horror as the only people who ate Tim's slop casserole were Candy Vargo and Tim. Everyone else had politely passed.

"While we wait for Gideon and Lilith to come back in, tell me about the Higher Power, please," Cecily repeated. *"Explain to me how It's different from God."*

On the tv, Candy Vargo pushed her clean plate aside, burped and popped a toothpick into her mouth.

"God's a human thing," the *Keeper of Fate* explained.

"So, the Bible isn't true?" Cecily asked.

I watched as past-me leaned forward, elbows on the table, as I perked with interest. I remember thinking that the Demon Goddess had read my mind and had asked for answers to the same theological mysteries that had stumped me since my life as the Death Counselor had begun.

"You wanna take this one, Angel?" Candy asked Cher.

Cher was Cecily's talent agent who happened to be an ancient Angel. The tiny woman was very heavy-handed with the makeup but lovely in an over-the-top way. She and Candy Vargo were friends who went waaaaaaay back.

"You betcha," Cher replied, taking a swig off her wine cooler then *dabbing at her mouth with a Versace hanky. "Plenty of truth in it. Plenty of untruths. You know when you play telephone?"*

Everyone nodded.

"Well, that's kinda how it came to be. Short version, in my opinion, is this—stories got told and passed on repeatedly over the years— some got embellished, some got forgotten. Then they decided to write it all down in what would be recognized as a dead language today," Cher explained.

Watching our past come to life on a TV from Charlie's magic was surreal. Even so, I didn't know what any of this had to do with our current situation, but I also trusted that Charlie wouldn't be showing this to me if it wasn't somehow important. At least, some of it. I reminded myself to be patient, something I didn't have a lot of. Some of the information was bound to be extraneous, and while I wished the Immortals around me would learn how to use bullet points, that wasn't the way it worked. The important parts would be revealed when the time was right. I felt it in my gut.

"Oh yes!" Tim said. "It was eventually translated by men into Latin then later into other languages."

"Men who might or might not have had different agendas," Charlie explained. *"Basically, the game of telephone continued."*

"Women were not involved," Heather added, pointedly. "Therefore, Immortals tend to look at the Bible as a collection of stories that make an attempt to lead humankind to do good."

"But them fuckers have taken the bits and the pieces that support their own beliefs. Bottom line is that God is love. Period. If all the

fuckbuckets in the world would just abide by that they'd be a whole lot better off," Candy said flatly.

"Charlie, pause that shit for a hot sec," Candy yelled.

Charlie obliged.

"I come off really fuckin' smart!" Candy Vargo announced proudly.

"You'd come off a lot smarter without all them F-bombs," Gram commented.

Jolly Sue cleared her throat. "Normally, I'd agree that an individual who uses profanity as much as Candy Vargo is a bawdy, crook-plated hussy. However, in Candy's case I shall excuse her and simply call her a pribbling lewdster."

Dimple punched Jolly Sue in the head. Not much damage happened since they were ghosts. "I wouldn't go that far. I believe Candy Vargo is a gleeting canker-blossom. Much milder," Dimple said.

Lura Belle was annoyed. "I am TRYING to watch TV," she hissed at her dead posse. "You are both haggard fat-kidneyed, nut-hooks. Time is wasting. We must focus on how to save the day. It's unclear how much time we have left."

Both Jolly Sue and Dimple hung their heads.

"Charlie," Lura Belle called out. "Please do your voodoo so we can glean the knowledge. The beslubbering hedge pigs will not interrupt again."

"Correct," Dimple chimed in. "However, I'd like to end the conversation by informing everyone that Lura Belle is a cock-ered, weedy strumpet."

The three dead dummies jumped each other and went to town. The punches weren't exactly landing, but the turn-of-the-century insults sure were. Their ghostly fists went right through their targets. When I tried to break up the fight, I got called currish, lumpish, humper-mugger. I was done. Picking them up since I could physically touch the dead, I tossed them out into the front yard.

"Boys," I called out to the queens. "Do you mind refereeing a smackdown?"

"Would luuurve it, girlfriend," Fred assured me, galloping over on his steed. "What seems to be the problem?"

"No problem," I told him. "Just normal Lura Belle-Jolly Sue-Dimple behavior. I've found it best to let them get it out of their systems. Just make sure if they lose any appendages, they hang onto them so I can glue them back together."

"Will do, Sugar Pants," Wally squealed. He was always down for a little violence.

With a wave to the queens, I walked back into the house and sat back down. "Charlie, can we resume?'

"Absolutely," he said. Charlie clapped his hands and the scene continued.

"So, God is real?" Cecily pressed, clearly confused.

The Keeper of Fate shrugged. "Depends on what you wanna believe, Badass. Many bloody wars amongst the humans have been fought in the name of religion. Some ain't never gonna end. Not real fucking sure if that's what God would have intended."

"Not helping," Cecily said to Candy.

She shrugged. "Not trying to. Some questions have no answers. Some have millions of answers. Faith is a choice."

"Moving on," Cecily stated. "The Higher Power. Explain."

Abaddon, Cecily's handsome Demon mate, joined the discussion. "The Higher Power is more of an entity than a being—an elusive light. Smoke and mirrors—danger, love and wickedness personified. Not something to be questioned or called on. The Universe is neither black nor white. It's gray. The Higher Power could also be considered gray."

Cecily squinted at him. "There's a problem."

He raised a brow and waited.

"I'm about to call on It. And I have a lot of questions. You just said that's a no-no."

Abaddon held up a hand. "You're not calling on It to come to you. You're going to It. You're not questioning the existence of It. You're demanding specific answers to a specific situation. Words are made to be interpreted in many ways. Keep that in mind."

Charlie waved his hand in a circular motion and the images sped up. "This next part is irrelevant."

"Wait!" Candy griped. "Ain't this the part where Tim tells Cecily to pinch her weenus and she thinks he means penis?"

I chuckled despite myself. The weenus-penis convo had been undeniably funny.

"So embarrassing," Tim lamented, blushing.

"It was fuckin' hilarious," she insisted.

Charlie gave Candy the side eye. That shut her up fast. No one wanted to piss off Charlie. "It is, and we're skipping it. It has no pertinent intel on the Higher Power and Cecily could arrive any moment. I'd suggest we only watch what's necessary.

"I agree," I said, trying not to snicker. "Everyone, zip it and watch.

Cecily glanced around the room. "Has anyone actually seen It?"

"With our eyes?" Charlie asked.

"Yep. Eyes," she confirmed.

"That ain't how you see the Higher Power," Candy Vargo volunteered.

Abaddon, who seemed to sense that Cecily's patience was wearing thin, spoke up. "Think of it like an immersive experience."

"Like one of those water tanks where you get all weightless and shit," Cher chimed in.

"Not really," Abaddon said. "It's a state of mind. Sort of."

Cher clapped excitedly. "Like wearing those fancy VD goggles the kids love these days."

"Are there goggles for venereal diseases?" Tim asked with a horrified expression.

Candy flicked a toothpick at him. "She means VR goggles. Virtual reality, not a sexually transmitted disease." She sniffed. "It ain't a half-bad notion."

Cher preened at her buddy's compliment, her green and red lips smacking as she grinned.

Cecily shook her head. "Unless someone actually has goggles that will get me where I need to go, this is really unhelpful. Okay. Let me try again. Where is the Higher Power?"

"On a different plane," Tim said. "Similar to the Darkness and the Light, but different."

"Do we transport there?" she asked.

No one spoke.

Cecily tried again. "Like to the different plane? Do we transport?"

Silence.

"Let's break this down." Cecily began to pace the room. "Either no one knows the answers, or you're not allowed to share. However, I have Pandora inside of me, and I want her out. If there's another way to do that, I'm all ears. If that's not the case, then I have to get to the Higher Power, and I would seriously appreciate some layman's instructions."

Lilith, Cecily's mother and the former Goddess of the Darkness, walked back into the scene with Gideon beside her. She joined the conversation. "You will be able to commune with the Higher Power as the Goddess of the Darkness."

"Wait. Hold up." Cecily's hands doubled into fists at her sides, but she kept her tone calm and reasonable. "Is the Higher Power actually a person? Someone or thing that's tangible? All of you guys keep saying It's an entity... you can't see It with your eyes. Bottom line,

I'm fucking confused. How can you talk to something that's been described to me as an elusive light?"

Candy Vargo blew a loud raspberry from her mouth. "Shit's hard to comprehend," she admitted. "Don't help all that fuckin' much that you're only forty years old."

"I'm also forty," I'd reminded everyone. "I stand with Cecily on this line of questioning. She and I have accepted a lot in a short amount of time. The Higher Power is difficult to swallow. Not to mention, Cecily has to deal with It. Soon. Enough of the vague bull-shit. If no one here knows what they're talking about, admit it. Give the Bitch Goddess Cecily the respect she's due. All of you are old enough, and I do mean old enough, to acknowledge if you have no clue how to explain this."

The room went silent. Glances were exchanged.

Gideon was the one to speak first. Bowing his head in respect to both Cecily and me, he smiled apologetically. "As usual, the Angel of Mercy speaks with common sense that us older people seem to have forgotten how to use. Sometimes to make clear what is muddy can verge on impossible."

"Nothing is impossible," I reminded the man I loved. "You just have to believe."

"Great fucking monologue," Candy Vargo said, clapping me on the back. "You come off as pretty smart yourself."

Gram didn't even yell at her for the foul language as she zipped around above. "That's my girl," she preened. "Always has been the smartest gol'darn person in the room."

I'll admit it felt good, making Gram proud.

"There's more to watch," Charlie said, unpausing the shit-show of our past with a wave of his hand.

On-screen Gideon chuckled. "Fine," he said to on-screen me. "The Higher Power is whatever or whomever you see It as."

Cecily rolled her eyes. I didn't blame her. "Soooooo, if I want Tim to be the Higher Power because he's really nice then he becomes the Higher Power?"

Tim giggled. "Oh my! What a lovely compliment, Bitch Goddess Cecily! But alas, no. It doesn't work that way."

"Lemme give it a shot," Candy Vargo said.

"Be my guest, friend," Tim told her.

"Alrighty then," she said, splaying her hands out in front of her. She began to shimmer and her knotted hair floated around her head. It was a scary look coupled with her mismatched sweats and sandals. "Pretend you're on the Higher Power's plane."

"How did I get there?" Cecily asked.

Candy hissed at her. "That don't matter right yet."

Cecily took a healthy step back. "Got it."

"Just envision what I'm fuckin' sayin', Badass," she instructed. "You're just fuckin' walking along and minding your own business, and then BAM! You feel It. Your blood runs cold, and you sneeze like a motherfucker. All of a sudden, the wind kicks up and the trees uproot—screamin' in agony as they break in half like they were twigs. The animals begin to screech, and the air smells of death. You close your eyes, and all of a sudden Mr. Fucking Rogers is standing there with Mr. McFeely. You're pretty sure that Pee-wee Herman is nearby since his bike is hanging from one of the trees."

"Oh my God. STOP," Heather snapped. She was glowing, and her magical tattoos raced along her arms and neck. "With all due respect, what in the actual fuck are you talking about? Not real sure this is helping."

Candy raised her hands to electrocute Heather. Heather was ready to go back at the Keeper of Fate with her hands held high. Abaddon stepped between the women and growled.

"Stand down," he ground out. "Violence is not what is needed. Do you understand or shall we take this outside so I can help you understand?"

Both women dropped their arms. The entire room heaved a sigh of relief.

Lilith began to laugh. It sounded unhinged, but it was definitely laughter. "Hang on, please. I have to disagree with Heather. Candy Vargo has made a fine point—rather bizarre, but not unhelpful."

Everyone stared at Lilith.

"Keep talking," Cecily told her mother.

"Open the door in your mind and let Pandora join the conversation," she instructed. "But give her a warning that the door can be bolted shut again as easily as it was unbolted."

We couldn't hear Pandora, not then or now, since in the scene she was trapped inside of Cecily's mind. Unfortunately, from the pained wince on Cecily's face she could hear the evil goddess loud and clear.

"You are not in charge, Pandora. I am. If you want to be released, then I'd highly suggest you swallow the bile in your foul mouth and participate in a reasonably polite manner."

Cecily was silent as she listened to the crazed woman she was housing inside her against her will.

"Dude," Cecily snapped. "You don't even have a freaking body at the moment. You are in no position to negotiate. I've locked you out once, and I can do it again. This time I'll throw the key into the abyss. In other words, it's my way or the highway."

Even though we couldn't hear Pandora, she could hear us. Cecily nodded to her mother to speak.

"Tell Cecily what you know of the Higher Power," Lilith said.

Cecily was quiet as she listened to Pandora's answer.

"She said the questions have to be more specific," Cecily told us, then immediately jumped back in and questioned Pandora herself. "How do I get to the Higher Power?" She paused and listened to the voice only she could hear. "She says, to get to the Higher Power, I have to be in a dream state."

"Interesting," Tim said. "Makes sense."

"It does," Lilith agreed, shaking her head in wonder. "I'd never thought of it like that."

"Sounds random," Cecily said. "I mean, is it like the freaking Wizard of Oz where I need to get caught in a tornado or Alice in Wonderland and fall through a hole?"

"Careful there, girlie," Candy Vargo warned, looking nervous which was rare for her. "Words got too much power in our world. My experience with the Higher Power looked like it did because I watch too many fuckin' horror movies along with kids' shows."

Cecily looked alarmed. Hell, we were all alarmed. "Who here has actually been in the presence of the Higher Power? Raise your hands, please."

As expected, Candy Vargo and Lilith raised their hands.

Gideon was the only other Immortal in the room to raise his hand.

"Welp, I kind of know how to get there in a roundabout and ambiguous way," Cecily said. "Moving on. Pandora, what does the Higher Power look like... to you?"

Again, Cecily listened. Her brow was wrinkled in thought as Pandora spoke to her.

"What did she say?" Charlie asked.

"True beauty," Cecily repeated. "Apparently, it's a combo of Brad Pitt, Warren Beatty, Dolly Parton, Clark Gable and I think the last one was Jennifer Aniston."

"Jesus," Candy muttered. "That's a lot tamer than my version."

"Word," Cecily replied. "Lilith, tell me your version, please."

"Nirvana," she replied. "Wildly colored flowers, vines and trees— nature at its' explosive finest. Absolute peace and tranquility."

"What the fuck?" Candy griped. "Not what I saw."

Cecily ignored Candy and focused on her mom. "That's what the Higher Power looks like to you?" she questioned.

Lilith shook her head. "I can't say I've seen the Higher Power in any kind of form with my eyes. For me, it's the place where the Higher Power resides. My communication was through nature. No words were necessary."

And the information kept getting more bewildering.

"Gideon," Cecily said, sounding a little desperate at this point. "What about you?"

"More like what Candy Vargo experienced."

"You saw Pee-wee Herman?" Candy demanded.

"No," he said, flatly. "It was full of devastation and death. Very dark, rigged with land mines and not a place I'd like to revisit."

"Seems to me, it's the state of mind the person is in as to what they see," Charlie observed as Heather nodded her agreement.

"I concur," Heather said. "Cecily, as random as this advice might seem, stay positive. Don't let your mind go to any dark depths."

She nodded her agreement. "Next. Is it possible to die in a dream state?"

"Excellent question," the Grim Reaper said. "And the answer is no. You can be killed but you won't die. Although, that means anything you kill in the dream state isn't dead either. Keep that in mind. If you kill an enemy there, you will have to end your enemy multiple times."

"Am I going to have to kill shit there? Will there be things on the Higher Power's plane that want me dead?" Cecily asked.

"Up to you," Candy Vargo explained. "It's your fuckin' dream state, Badass."

"Got it. Another question, how do I get back from the dream state?"

"Click your heels three times," Candy suggested.

Heather zapped her. Candy zapped her back.

As I watched, I remembered thinking that Cecily didn't need the two Immortals going after each other, not when so much was at stake. So, I'd put myself between them and had given them a withering look that made both of them blanch.

"*Do not make me have to put either of you in time out,*" on-screen *me warned, eyeing them steadily. "You will not enjoy it."*

"*Sorry," Heather said, pulling Candy back to her feet. "Knee-jerk reaction to Candy being an idiot."*

The Keeper of Fate chuckled. "Might be an idiot, but that's how I got back."

"*Seriously?" Cecily asked. "Like Dorothy in the Wizard of Oz?"* *Candy nodded.*

"*Mom? Gideon?" Cecily asked. "What about you guys?"*

"*For me, it wasn't conscious," Lilith admitted. "My body came back to this plane when the time was right."*

Gideon pressed the bridge of his nose and sighed. "I certainly hope this doesn't apply to you, Bitch Goddess Cecily, but I came back once I'd slayed the monster."

"*Fuck," she muttered and then was silent for a long moment. Clearly Pandora was speaking again. "Pandora said that while I can't die in the dream state, I could get stuck there."*

Lilith nodded slowly. "I've always understood that to be true. It's the reason I've only gone to the plane of the Higher Power a few times in my millions of years."

Cecily wasn't done. "Is there a time limit? A tangible one of how long I can stay without getting trapped there?"

Gideon answered. "Not as far as I'm aware. However, get out as quickly as you can. Time runs differently on different planes."

"Well, that's certainly a neat trick," a familiar voice said from behind us.

I whipped around and was shocked that none of us had noticed their entrance. That didn't bode well for us being on top of our game. The Bitch Goddess Cecily had arrived. As expected, she was accompanied by Abaddon. What wasn't expected and wasn't welcome was the third person in the group.

Gideon growled. The sound came from deep in his throat and made goosebumps pop up on my arms. Charlie wasn't pleased either, and his power began to fill the room. I took short, shallow breaths so I didn't pass out. Giving my friend a pained glance, he nodded in apology and tamped back the magic. Tim walked across the room and placed himself next to me. Gram and Mr. Jackson joined Tim.

Only Candy Vargo seemed unsurprised by Pandora's presence.

"Why is that disgusting waste of humanity here?" Gideon demanded in a tone so vicious everyone grew even more tense.

Cecily stepped in front of Pandora with a calm expression on her stunning face. "She's changed."

"Bullshit," Gideon hissed as his eyes glowed bright red in fury. "With all due respect, you've been the Goddess of the Darkness for a month, Cecily. You have no concept of the vileness of the woman standing next to you." His gaze landed on Pandora. If looks could kill she would have been dead.

Pandora moved out from behind Cecily and met Gideon's menacing scowl. "I don't blame you for your hatred, Grim Reaper," she said in a flat tone. "And to be honest, while I might have changed a bit, I'm still the horrific person I've always been deep down. However, if you want to deal with the Higher Power, I'm the one to help."

"I'd rather chew glass and swallow it than accept help from someone like you," Gideon shot back. His eyes were now shooting sparks, and I prepared for his ebony black wings to explode from his back.

Jennifer started to come back down the stairs with Alana Catherine, took one look at the unfolding scene and promptly turned around and hightailed it back upstairs. My human buddy was smart.

Cecily joined the conversation. Abaddon stayed quiet. "Pandora is wrong about her character, but that's neither here nor there," she stated, giving the woman next to her a pointed glare. "We can apprise you of what happened on the Higher Power's plane, but I'm on Its hit list at the moment. If you need someone with recent experience, then Pandora is the person you're searching for."

None of that sounded like a good plan. Pandora was one of the most evil Immortals in existence. The trail of death and destruction she'd left behind was long and horrifying. She'd destroyed lives for millions of years. Gideon despised her. I didn't know Cecily well enough to completely trust her, but right now it didn't look like we had much of a choice."

Shit.

Inhaling deeply and exhaling slowly, I decided to have an exploratory conversation-interrogation. My options were... hell, I didn't know what my options were. All I knew was that I had to somehow fix a tear in the Light. How to do it was anyone's guess. And since no one had a guess, I was going to deal with what I was given.

Double shit.

I didn't know if this was a gift or a disaster waiting to happen. There was only one way to find out.

Pandora's gaze roved over the room and landed on my plant table. Internally, I winced. Outwardly, I was blasé. It had been the beginnings of a new hobby that had failed miserably. Every single plant was brown, crunchy and dead. I'd been meaning to toss them, but my insane life had gotten in the way.

Pandora's brow rose and she smirked. Her gaze moved to

mine in challenge. "Why do you have houseplants if you kill them, Angel of Mercy?"

Challenge accepted. I smiled at her and winked. "To remind everyone what I'm capable of, Goddess of the Darkness."

Her eyes grew wide along with everyone else's in the room. If Pandora thought she could fuck around, she was about to find out. I played to win. If she could help me, so be it. If she couldn't, she was out of here.

"Shall we get started?" I asked flatly.

"Hell to the fuckin' yes!" Candy Vargo shouted. She ushered Cecily, Abaddon and Pandora to one side of the room, while directing the rest of us to the other. "It's time to get this party started!"

Cecily frowned. "Hey, that's my line."

Candy gave her a sheepish grin.

Whatever. I wasn't sure I'd call it a party, but it was definitely time to get started.

CHAPTER FIVE

I EXPLAINED TO OUR GUESTS WHAT WAS GOING ON. CECILY WAS disturbed by the story of the dead who had been in the Light coming back. What she and Abaddon were more disturbed about was the message from Agnes.

"Repeat what Agnes said, please," Cecily insisted tightly.

I nodded gratefully when Tim handed me his notepad. While I recalled what my dead friend had said, I needed to be sure. Tim was the absolute best with his anal note taking.

"She said, *Fix the rift in the chain, Angel of Mercy. If unattended, evil from the Darkness will descend on the earth and tear it open for good. Death and destruction will rule.*"

Cecily turned to Pandora. Her expression was pained but intense. I exchanged a quick look with Gideon, but his focus was on Pandora. His eyes still spit sparks but at least his wings hadn't emerged. A fight between some of the most powerful people in existence wouldn't end well. Right now, I was pissed that Cecily had brought Pandora. Nothing good could come of it. I had no intention of asking the Bitch Goddess Cecily to physically help us. All we wanted was information from her visit to the Higher Power's plane.

"Do you know anything about this?" Cecily asked Pandora. Her voice was calm, but it was steely underneath. She wasn't messing around.

Pandora had the gall to roll her eyes. I had to give it to her. No one in the room liked the Demon. Honestly, I wasn't sure anyone in the world liked her. Every Immortal here could likely end her. She didn't give a damn. Her tone was dripping in sarcasm. "Let's see... I was stuck inside of you after you turned me into what basically amounted to a mist. Then I went along for the most horrific ride I've ever taken. You turned all of my people against me and now I'm on probation and haven't been back to the Darkness. Not sure how you would surmise that I'm responsible for any of this."

Cecily sighed then nodded curtly. Pandora had made her point. This had nothing to do with her. However, none of this was pertinent to our cause.

"Moving on," I said in a tone that meant business. "What did the Higher Power look like?"

Cecily made a face. "It was a four-foot-nothing red-headed chain-smoker named Phyllis with a wise-guy vocabulary—New Jersey accent and all. However, that's not what you'll see. At least, I don't think it is."

She was probably right. The Higher Power looked different to each person who saw It. In a moment of clarity, I realized this conversation was moot. Nothing that applied to Cecily would apply to me other than how to get there. I already knew how to get there—a dream state.

"Shit," I muttered.

"I have thoughts," Pandora said.

"Well, that's fuckin' frightening," Candy Vargo announced.

The Keeper of Fate was ignored.

I stared at Pandora. The Demon Goddess stared right back. She had changed but could a leopard ever truly lose their spots? Trusting her was off the table, but I'd hear her out. "And they are?"

She smiled. It was scary. The woman was beautiful but as cold as ice. Gideon growled again and the smile left her lips. "It will cost you," she said.

The Immortals weren't big on owing favors, and it was never a good idea to owe anyone anything—especially someone like Pandora.

If she wanted to play games, I would play. Having no clue where to start to solve the problem wasn't a great place to be. Steve had said I only had days to figure out how to fix the rift. If Pandora was useful, I would pay. If the thoughts were bullshit…

"Fine," I said flatly as I heard all the Immortals in the room groan. "If you have something worth saying I'll pay. If you don't… you'll pay."

That gave the Demon pause. Cecily took her hand and held it. The kind gesture made Pandora squirm, but she didn't pull away. It was beyond clear that Cecily believed in her. Why? I didn't know, but that wasn't my problem.

"Fine," Pandora hissed. "No payment." She rolled her eyes again. Twice. "I think It is testing us—all of us."

I squinted at her and said nothing.

She continued. "I think that It wanted to make sure the Goddesses of the Darkness would work in somewhat of a harmony," she said, then sighed dramatically. "It is an idiot. However, if that was the plan then it worked to a certain degree."

Mulling that over, I glanced around the room. Cecily and

Abaddon exchanged loaded glances. Charlie was pensive. Tim scribbled notes like his life depended on it. Candy Vargo had shoved her hands into her pockets and was looking up at the ceiling. Gideon was still staring daggers at Pandora. The ghosts were silent.

"Possibly," I said. "But that makes no sense for our situation."

Pandora shrugged. "That's why I decided not to charge. Either It is trying to fix things or Armageddon is coming."

And on that lovely note, the Four Horsemen of the Apocalypse came galloping through the front door—or what used to be the front door. It was kind of shocking. The steeds were breathing hard like they'd just run the Kentucky Derby. The boys were all done up and didn't appear pleased—fangs out, horns on fire and still in sequin gowns from the wedding. Dimple rode with Dirk. Lura Belle rode with Wally and Jolly Sue rode with Fred. They looked a little worse for the wear. Carl rode alone.

As they dismounted, Cecily, Abaddon and Pandora took a few steps back. Clearly, it was the first time they'd met the harbingers of the end times...

"Hey," Candy Vargo grunted, pointing at the queens. "I meant what I said about them horses shittin' in the house. They poop, you eat."

Dirk waved his hand and the massive horses trotted back outside. There was no smile on my buddy's face. His expression was grim. The four queens stood shoulder to shoulder. Their gazes roamed the great room. When they landed on Pandora, they stayed.

"Interesting you should mention Armageddon," Carl said coldly. "You've done your very best to bring it on, I'd think you would have stated that with far more joy, *Goddess*."

The Horsemen were not silly or fun right now. They were angry. Part of me worried for Pandora's safety. However, an imbalance in the Immortal world wasn't something that anyone wanted—even the queens. That would hasten the end times by a hell of a lot.

"I've always wanted to meet you," Dirk told the Goddess with an expression of utter disdain. "It's quite fascinating to observe how such impressive beauty was given to one so vile."

Wally laughed. It held no humor whatsoever. Pandora looked like she wanted to be anywhere but here. Why in the hell did I feel bad for her? I was losing my marbles. Yes, I was the Angel of Mercy, but from everything I knew, the woman had shown no mercy to anyone in millions of years.

"You're repulsive," Wally said calmly. He didn't raise his voice. "It's academically interesting to see you standing there with no shame. I feel filthy in your presence."

It was strange to hear such horrible words doled out as if he were discussing the weather. It made his words cut faster and deeper. Pandora, whose head had been held high, now stared at the floor.

After a long moment, she raised her chin. "You are not inside me," she said with no emotion in her voice. "You have no idea what I feel."

Fred was having none of it. "And do you care what you've made hundreds of thousands of others feel?" he demanded through clenched teeth.

I was aware that very little in our world happened without reason, but for the life of me I couldn't find one good reason for what was happening now. At the rate it was going the next part of the scene would have carnage in it.

Stepping forward, I held up a hand. "This is not the time or the place for Pandora's trial," I said. "There's a tear in the Light.

I have to fix it. All I wanted was some information about the Higher Power's plane. That info isn't mine to be had." I ran my hands through my hair in frustration. "I'm just going to wing it. It's worked so far."

"'So far' means that eventually it won't," Cecily said.

Walking over to the wooden table with the dead plants on it, I knocked on it. Hard. The brown crunchy leaves fell from the dead stems and floated to the floor. "Not going to give that any energy," I told her. "Thank you for coming. I'm sorry we wasted your time."

"Daisy!" Jennifer called from the top of the stairs. "Are your sparkly magic friends still here?"

Pandora, Cecily and Abaddon appeared confused. Even from Jennifer's voice it was obvious she was human.

"They are," I called back. "Is everything okay?"

Gideon was at the bottom of the stairs in less time than it took to blink. He didn't screw around when it came to our daughter.

"It's fabu! Our little pooper is brilliant!" Jennifer squealed. "A first just happened and y'all missed it. I'm coming down. Y'all are not gonna believe it!"

My stomach dropped. I was in the middle of what could amount to the end of everything and I was more devastated that I'd missed one of my daughter's firsts.

Jennifer hustled down the stairs with a babbling, beautiful baby in her arms. The Four Horsemen were not happy with the company and moved to create a drag queen wall, separating Cecily, Abaddon and Pandora from our child.

"Is that a human?" Pandora asked warily. "A human who is aware of the Immortal world?"

Jennifer waved. "Sure am, but don't worry yourself about it!

Name's Jennifer and I'm real dang good at keeping secrets! And... here's the kicker, I've got so much Botox in my face, I'm invincible. Also had my boobs and ass done. Got a buttload of botulism and filler in me. Cost me the settlements from a couple of my divorces. If I get hit by a magic zinger it just bounces right off."

Cecily laughed with delight. "Is she serious?"

"Very," I replied then turned back to the Botoxed gal in question. "What did my baby do?" I took Alana Catherine into my arms and sniffed her little head. I had no idea why babies and puppies smelled so delicious, but I was going to enjoy it for as long as I could.

Jennifer tried to grin, but the filler in her face made it difficult. "She said, papa!"

Gideon looked like he was about to cry with happiness. If I was being honest, I was the tiniest bit jealous that mama wasn't her first word, but my excitement overrode any petty crap I felt.

"That there baby is as smart as a whip," Gram said, floating over. "Kinda young to be talkin' but that ain't surprising considerin' who her mama and daddy are!"

Gram had a point. It was way too early for Alana to be talking. She wasn't even sitting up yet. However, the point had been well made. Her daddy was the Grim Reaper and her mama was the Angel of Mercy slash Death Counselor. Weird was our normal.

"Papa," Alana Catherine said, pointing her chubby finger across the room.

"He's right here, baby," I cooed at her as Gideon stepped into her sightline.

"Papa," she said again, not looking at Gideon. She wagged her little finger towards where the queens stood.

I laughed. "Umm… those are your well-dressed uncles," I told her. "Papa is right here." I handed her to Gideon.

He kissed her nose and cuddled her close. Our daughter wasn't having any of it. She kept pointing across the room and babbling papa over and over.

Candy Vargo walked over and reached out for the baby. "May I?"

Gideon gave her a stern look that would have made most people run and hide. It didn't faze Candy. "May you what?"

"Can I have the baby so we can fuckin' figure out what she's tryin' to tell us?" she shot right back.

Everyone winced at her choice of words. Even Candy Vargo grimaced.

"Lemme try that again," she muttered.

"That's right," Gram chastised her. "If the F-bomb is the next thing out of that baby's mouth, I'm gonna pitch a hissy fit with a tail on it. Once we get this settled, you and me are goin' into the bathroom and you're gonna wash that mouth out with soap. Three times! You hear me, girlie?"

"Why three?" Tim asked Gram.

Gram shrugged. "Three has power," she told him. "Always been my favorite number."

Tim jotted it down.

"Did you hear me, Candy girl?" Gram demanded.

"Yes, ma'am," Candy said contritely. "My bad." She took a deep breath and tried again. "Gideon, can you hand me the baby so that I can freakin' figure out what she's wantin' to say?"

I nodded at Gideon. Candy Vargo would sooner chop off her own head than let something happen to our child. Getting our daughter involved was not anywhere on the agenda, but since there was very little to nothing on the list of how to fix the mess we were in, it kind of didn't surprise me.

Candy gently took Alana Catherine into her arms and kissed the top of her head. "Alrighty then, little cutie pie, tell Auntie Candy who you want to talk to."

Alana Catherine pulled on Candy's hair with one hand and pointed across the room with the other. "Papa," she squealed with a giggle. "Papa!"

As Candy Vargo walked across the room, the queens parted so she could get through the Immortal wall. I followed close behind with Gideon. Had the ghosts come back? Did my child sense them? Eventually—hopefully a very long time from now—she would take over for me as the Death Counselor. The gift ran in our bloodline. She was already very aware of the dead and adored them.

Her shrieking got louder and louder as she got closer to where Cecily, Abaddon and Pandora stood. I could feel my body tense as it became clear that papa didn't mean daddy. It meant Pandora. However, no one was as shocked as the woman in question. She stepped back in terror.

"Hmm…" Candy Vargo said, shaking her head in surprise. "This is some weird shi…"

"Candy Vargo," Gram shouted in warning. "You watch your mouth around my great grandbaby!"

"I meant it's a weird shiiiituation," she said, trying to save her ass and failing. "Alana Catherine wants to talk to Pandora."

"Absolutely not," Gideon ground out.

I touched his shoulder to calm him. "I don't like it either, but as I've been told repeatedly, never say no to a gift."

His body was as wound up as a bomb about to go off. I wasn't too far behind, but maybe the reason why Cecily,

Abaddon and Pandora were here was for this very moment. Or… I'd lost the rest of my debatably sane mind.

"I'll solve this by leaving," Pandora announced loudly. "I'm not fit to be touched by a child."

Candy Vargo chuckled. "First time I've ever agreed with you, jackass," she said. "But you ain't goin' nowhere until this little gal is satisfied."

"I beg to differ," Pandora snapped.

The Keeper of Fate bounced the future Death Counselor in her arms and eyed Pandora. The Demon Goddess squirmed under her gaze. "I'm gonna ask you a few questions, and you're gonna answer them."

Pandora sighed dramatically but didn't backtalk Candy Vargo. No one but Gram got away with backtalking her. The Keeper of Fate was the original badass. She knew it. We knew it, and Pandora definitely knew it.

"Tell me what you think about the Higher Power," Candy said.

Pandora didn't miss a beat. "I'd go to Its funeral, but not to Its birthday party."

I laughed. It was impossible not to. The side of the Demon Goddess' lip quirked up. She was aware she'd made a good one.

"Next," Candy Vargo said with a grin. "Figure this one out. I'm the fuckin' piece of string that joins the divide, the delicate place where hope resides. I can start with a spark, a fiery flame to light up the dark. Alone, I stumble, destined to fall. Together, we can conquer all. What in the hell am I?"

"Insane?" Pandora guessed.

I had to bite my lip to keep myself from laughing again. The Demon Goddess was a comedienne on a roll.

"Yep," Candy agreed. "But that's well known. Answer the riddle, idiot."

The word *riddle* jumped out at me. Steve's words danced in my mind—'You have only days to discover the riddle and solve it. Start with the ending you desire and work your way back. It's the only way. Remember nothing is impossible… you just have to believe.' The riddle was important. I had a bad feeling this entire mission would be filled with them.

"You're Belief," Pandora said with annoyance. "And you're wasting my time."

Candy Vargo's eyes narrowed. Pandora stepped back. Alana Catherine blew a raspberry and giggled while pulling on Auntie Candy's hair. "I never waste time," she said flatly. "You need to remember that fuc…arkin' riddle because you need it more than anyone here."

"That was close," Gram muttered, giving Candy the eyeball.

Candy spared Gram a glance and a grin. "Sure was, Gram. Hey, Mailman," she said to Tim. "I'd like it to be noted that I avoided the word fuck!"

"Until now," I said with a wince. When the day came, I'd have to sit Alana Catherine down and explain the difference between language that we used and language that Candy used. Our language—good. Candy's language—bad.

"Anyhoo," Candy said in her outdoor voice, quickly moving on before Gram made her go to the bathroom and start washing her potty mouth out with soap. "Cecily believes in you. Don't know how many others do since you used to be a gaping hole of death and destruction. You have your work cut out for you. But you ain't gonna get real far unless you believe in yourself."

It took everything Pandora had not to roll her eyes. It was fascinating to watch. She shook her head and opened her mouth. No words came out. She tried again and failed.

"Papa!" Alana Catherine said softly, reaching for the Demon Goddess. "Papa."

Candy Vargo chuckled. "This here little nugget believes in you too. That makes three."

Pandora's head cocked to the side. "You need work on your math."

"My math is just fuc...aling fine, shithead." Candy stared at Pandora long and hard. Pandora held the Keeper of Fate's gaze. "I'm the third."

A small collective gasp filled the room. Pandora's was the loudest.

"You're a fool," she said.

"Been called worse," Candy admitted. "But I see a spark of something and I ain't never wrong. Truth hurts. Wear it."

I was sure Pandora wanted to refute everything Candy Vargo had just said. But she was wise and simply pressed her lips together.

She finally spoke. "What is she?" The Demon Goddess pointed at Alana Catherine.

"A baby," I said. "She's a baby."

She might not give Candy Vargo an eye roll, but she sure gave me one. "I can see that," she snapped. "That's not what I meant. Is she Immortal?"

"She is," Gideon answered coolly. He was doing his best not to attack Pandora. My husband was having a tough time of it. "My child will eventually become the Death Counselor. And let me be clear, if you ever harm even one single hair on her head, I will destroy you. Your demise will take decades and be filled with more pain and agony than your tiny little mind could imagine."

Pandora looked at him with dead eyes. "I'd deserve no less.

You have nothing to fear, Reaper. I will not harm the child. Ever."

Gideon nodded. It was jerky and filled with fury, but he didn't physically go at her. I considered it a win.

"PAPA!" Alana Catherine yelled, reaching for the Goddess of the Darkness.

"The child has spoken," Candy said. "She wants you to hold her."

I swallowed hard then swallowed again. It sounded like a gulp. I supposed it was. This was not in any scenario I'd ever imagined.

But here we were...

I wasn't sure I wanted to be at this party, but there was no way I was leaving.

CHAPTER SIX

PANDORA TREMBLED AS SHE HELD OUT HER ARMS. I'D NEVER SEEN anyone so uncomfortable around a baby. I was worried she'd drop her. Out of pure motherly instinct, I moved closer, ready to catch my daughter if she fell. The Demon spared me a grateful glance. It slightly calmed my frayed nerves.

Cecily put her hand on Pandora's back, and Abaddon stood by. The Demon hadn't said a word, but his presence spoke volumes. He was here for Cecily. I wasn't sure if he trusted Pandora, but he did trust Cecily.

Candy Vargo was all over the shiiiituation. As she placed my daughter into Pandora's arms, she positioned her so she was safe and secure. Gideon's stressed breathing was loud in the quiet room. His unease was evident. I wasn't relaxed, but wasn't as on edge. What was happening was nuts, but Alana Catherine was insistent and persistent.

I marveled at the bizarre circumstances unraveling in front of my eyes. Going from widowed paralegal, to the Death Counselor, to the Angel of Mercy, to being a mom was almost unthinkable. However, it was my truth. I was handling it the best I could. Seeing my daughter being held by one of the Goddesses of the Darkness had not been on my bingo card. It wouldn't alarm me to have the Bitch Goddess Cecily hold my baby, but it was surreal to see Pandora cradle my child. I was ready to snatch her back at the first sign of my child's distress.

"What do I do?" Pandora whispered, looking down at Alana Catherine like she was an alien.

"Nothin'," Candy Vargo said, pulling out a toothpick and popping it into her mouth. "You let her do what she wants to do. She's a special little chickadee, and I ain't got no clue why she wants you."

The Four Horsemen were still grim-faced, but they watched with curiosity. Lura Belle, Jolly Sue, and Dimple floated nearby, along with Gram and her beau, Mr. Jackson. Charlie stayed close to Gideon. That was smart. Charlie could handle him. Heck, Charlie could handle all of us. He was wise, kind, and powerful as they came. Tim and Jennifer were off to the side. Jennifer had a glass of wine, and Tim had his handy-dandy notebook.

We waited.

We didn't have to wait long.

Alana Catherine reached up and put her chubby hand on Pandora's cheek. My daughter giggled at the Goddess' startled expression.

"Is this okay?" Pandora choked out. "I mean, do I need to wash my face first? Don't you have to disinfect yourself to be around a baby?"

"It's fine. She's fine," I assured her. "Just relax."

Pandora appeared unsteady on her feet. I wasn't the only one who noticed. Without a word, Dirk brought over the armchair and placed it behind the anxiety-ridden woman. Cecily and Candy Vargo seated her. Alana Catherine was focused on papa—and only papa. Her small hand was still on her cheek, and she stared into the Demon's eyes.

"What?" Pandora asked, gaping at the baby in shock. "Again. Say that again."

There was some kind of silent communication going on. I was jealous. In vitro, my daughter could communicate with me. It had been a precious miracle. It had stopped soon after she was born.

"Three," Pandora recited.

"What about it?" Candy asked.

She shook her head and continued to stare at Alana Catherine. "Past, present and future."

Tim scribbled it all down. He didn't need to. I memorized every word.

"The game is a riddle. Three must play to win and break the evil spells," Pandora said. "The show will go on, and the wheels will turn. The answers are questions. The price must be right or the innocent will pay. In the end, the choice will be on the strongest. The strongest shall emerge the victor. Anything is possible. You just have to believe. Time is running out."

My stomach lurched. We were running out of time. That didn't work for me. I wasn't quite sure what the rest of the clues meant, but I got that one loud and clear.

"Three, three, three. No matter what she says, the number is three," Pandora repeated.

"Who is she?" I asked.

The Demon looked up. "You. She's talking about you."

Color me confused. I glanced over at Gideon. He wasn't as perplexed as I was. The love of my life seemed to understand, and he looked like he was about to implode. Now, my stomach was housing a marching band who'd eaten a vat of sugar before they went onto the field at halftime.

As I was about to ask more questions, Candy Vargo held up her hand. "After. We talk after. The chickadee is getting sleepy. It's almost over, Daisy."

She was right. Alana Catherine's eyes were getting heavy, and she stuck her thumb into her mouth. The look on Pandora's face was no longer one of terror. It was one of awe.

"I'm not sure I believe that," she said softly.

"What's that?" Tim asked, missing what she'd said.

"Nothing. I was speaking to the child."

"Spit it out," Candy Vargo said. "We need to hear all of it."

Pandora turned pink and appeared lost. "I think the last part was just for me."

Candy shook her head. "Nope. Whatever the little critter said is fair game. Out with it, or I'll yank it out of you."

That didn't sound good. Clearly, Pandora didn't think so either. With a put-upon sigh, she leaned forward and kissed Alana Catherine's head as the baby fell asleep. "She said that the path I'm walking will lead to salvation and that I'm free to leave now."

No one said a word. That was some heavy stuff. Tears rolled down Pandora's cheeks as she stood up and handed me my daughter. That didn't sound like something a future Death Counselor would know.

"She's very special," Pandora said, lightly touching Alana Catherine's cheek. "She's far more than anyone could imagine."

"Do you know?" I asked.

She shook her head. "I do not. The answers will come with time." The Goddess of the Darkness turned to her counterpart. "Bitch Goddess Cecily, the time has come for us to leave."

"Thank you," I said to Pandora. "I owe you."

She paused for a long moment. "No. I owe you. Take care of that baby."

"I will."

Cecily gave me a quick hug and wished me luck. Abaddon nodded curtly to all. Pandora was strangely subdued and thoughtful. They joined hands and disappeared in a shimmering black and red mist. We stood in silence for a few minutes after they'd disappeared. I wasn't sure what to make of the last part, but that would be dealt with eventually. Right now, we needed to decipher the clues. From the expression on Gideon's face, I didn't think I was going to like the answers.

"Alrighty fuckers," Candy Vargo announced. "Shit, I mean farkers. Let's get to work."

And we did.

I WAS NOT HAPPY. AFTER GOING BACK AND FORTH FOR AN HOUR, we'd worked out some of the puzzle. The answers were not satisfactory.

"Daisy girl," Gram said, hovering next to me as I held a still napping Alana Catherine in my arms. "You need to relax your crack."

"My crack is fine. It's my sanity that's the problem."

The debate had been heated. My baby had slept through the entire thing. Three meant the past, the present and the future. As in Death Counselors—Gram, me and Alana Catherine. The thought of taking my child to the Higher Power's plane was horrific. Plus, I wasn't sure logistically how it could be done. If I had to be in a dream state to get there, taking Gram and Alana Catherine didn't seem possible.

Anything was possible. I just had to believe. Those words, which usually calmed me, made me want to scream right now.

What I didn't want to *believe* was that I was supposed to put my baby in danger. Gideon was beside himself and had punched a few holes in the walls. If I hadn't been holding our child, I would have joined him.

"Look at it this way, darlin'," Gram continued. "Three's a right powerful number. You, me and that beautiful baby are the past, the present and the future. Kinda like the Holy Trinity of Death Counselors. The Father, the Son and I'm the Holy Ghost."

I groaned. While my bible knowledge was iffy, I knew about the Father, Son and Holy Ghost. "The genders are wrong," I pointed out.

"Times, they are a-changin'," she replied.

The room suddenly darkened. The sun streaming through the windows disappeared. A feeling of dread permeated the air. The four apocalyptic queens jumped to their feet and sprinted to the door in their stilettoes.

Handing Alana Catherine to Gideon I rushed over. "What?" I asked. "What's going on?"

Dirk took my hand and led me to the front yard. "Look up at that sky, sugar boot," he whispered.

I did. It looked wrong. Dark clouds rimmed in icy white sat high in the sky. They floated without grace and seemed to be sparring with each other. The wind was scented with something acrid and it grew cold quickly. Checking my watch, I realized it was only six. It shouldn't be getting dark yet. And it really shouldn't smell bitter and angry outside. "What is that?"

Wally shook his head and stared at the ominous sky. "Girlfriend, I'm not real sure. It needs to be dealt with, though."

My frustration was at an all-time high. I hadn't signed up for all of this world-ending shit, but it just kept landing in my freaking lap. "Is this a warning from the Higher Power?"

Candy Vargo joined the group on the lawn. "Well, fuck a

duck," she grumbled then went into her bossy mode. "Queens, I'm gonna suggest that you fuckers go on back to Kingdom Come and get out of town for a bit."

"Why?" I demanded. It felt safer with the Four Horsemen of the Apocalypse here with us.

"One, cause they ain't really supposed to be here. It might be their presence that's pissin' off the Higher Power. That's doubtful, though. Two, if Armageddon really is on the way, them boys are the only ones who can help stop it."

I squinted at her in confusion. "Is that what the bible says?"

She laughed. It was a tinny sound, and her smile didn't reach her eyes. "Hell to the no. It's what I say. Fate's what we make of it."

Fred mounted his steed and gave me a wistful smile. "I shall miss you, Daisy. No one in all of time has accepted us like you, your family and your friends. It's been a glorious blip in a long and mundane life."

Wally and Dirk hugged me and made a Daisy sandwich. It felt wonderful.

"Candy Vargo is correct, dollface. We have to go," Wally said, kissing my cheek then wiping away the lipstick smear he'd just left. "I shall leave you with this little tale. It might be useful. Many moons ago, I wanted to fit in with the human population and see what all the fuss was about. So, I took a job at a fast-food burger joint in Cleveland. It was so much fun!"

I had no idea where this was going. From the expression on Candy's face, she didn't either.

"Oh yes!" Dirk chimed in. "Wally had a fabulous uniform and everything! We found an empty house and lived there until some men in blue uniforms made us leave. Thrilling!"

"Those were the days," Carl recalled fondly. "Wally used to bring home burgers and fries every day! Delish!"

"Anyhoo, darlings," Wally went on. "I had this manager who was rather obsessed with making people feel small. It was just awful. She called herself Bunbun. I secretly called her Cow Bitch."

"She was a terrible one," Dirk chimed in. "Just dreadful."

"Does this fuckin' story have a point?" Candy asked.

I supported the question but not the way it was asked.

"Oh yes, honey pie!" Wally assured her. "You see, I also had this adorable friend at work named Lurba who enjoyed the burgers and fries as well. The little gal was poor as a church mouse, hilarious and painted my nails every Tuesday. The job at the burger place was heaven-sent for her. She needed it badly and was a very hard worker."

"Painted all of our nails," Carl reminded Wally. "As a token of our appreciation, we procured many trendy trinkets for the lovely Lurba. I cannot confirm or deny that Dirk may or may not have procured a vehicle for Lurba."

Dirk grinned shamelessly. "I can confirm it!"

I knew what procure meant. The queens had the stickiest fingers of anyone I knew. At the very least, it seemed as if they used their felonious ways for good.

"Luuuuurved her!" Fred said. "Lurba would put teeny tiny rhinestones on my nails."

"In the shape of an itty-bitty burger!" Carl squealed. "Brilliant!"

The sky was getting darker and stranger... just like this story.

"Soooooo," Wally said with tongue click and a snap of his well-manicured fingers. "Bunbun started making fun of Lurba. Told my darling Lurba that she was stupid and so poor that she had a tumbleweed for a pet. Said that she was trailer trash and that she was surprised that the bank hadn't repossessed the cardboard box Lurba lived in. Just mean."

"That Bunbun had no room to talk," Dirk huffed. "The woman looked like a dirty foot."

I was so confused and speechless. Candy Vargo appeared to be at a loss for words as well.

"Agreed," Wally said. "Bunbun used to do this when I wasn't around, but I found dear Lurba crying her eyes out on a two-for-one fry day in the ladies' loo. It broke my heart. Bunbun walked in on us and told my little buddy that she was so poor that she couldn't jump over a nickel to save a dime. I had no clue what that meant… still don't know what it means, but I knew it was hateful. Then she fired our little Luba, slapped her, took her uniform and tossed her out into the parking lot. That's when I lost it."

"Oh my hell," Candy muttered, getting interested in the story. "Did you kill her? Rip Bunbun's head off? Shove it up her ass? Throw her into the fryer?"

Wally was horrified. "Of course not. I didn't want to scare the other workers. I adored all of them, but had a sweet spot for Lurba. I just let Bunbun have it with words."

"So many words," Fred said with a thumbs up.

"Like?" I asked. I didn't want to be invested in the Bunbun and Lurba story since I had kind of a lot going on, but somehow, I was.

"Well, first, I got onto the intercom system so everyone could hear me. I told her that poor people could work their way up, but someone with a face like hers was stuck for life. There's no fixing butt-assed ugly!" Wally pumped his fists over his head. "Cow Bitch slunk away and never bothered anyone again."

"Don't forget you told Cow Bitch that she was so ugly that

when she looks in the mirror, her reflection screams and runs away!" Dirk reminded him.

"Oh!" Fred squealed. "You also made Bunbun aware that she was so unfortunate looking that even Hello Kitty said goodbye. The entire joint was cheering."

Wally continued to pump his fists in victory. I wasn't sure what the hell was even happening.

"All's well that ends well," Wally said, mounting his steed as the other queens followed suit. "We were able to procure a lot of money from a building that stores it, and set our lovely Lurba up with her very own nail salon—Lurba's Lacquer and Love. We still hit up the salon when we can get back to Cleveland. I just adore a teeny-tiny rhinestone burger!"

I didn't want to ask, but I had to... "What happened to Bunbun?"

Dirk giggled. Carl grinned. Fred pointed to Wally. Wally threw his head back and laughed. "Seems that Bunbun got arrested by those nice men in blue uniforms for a bank heist. She's serving ten to twenty in the Big House," Wally said with a smirk that made me laugh. "Would you like to know the moral of this tale, sugar lips?"

I nodded. It was most likely something that would matter. "Yes, please."

"Do. Not. Let. ANYONE fuck with the people you love. Ever," Wally said then blew me a kiss.

"Until we meet again, darlings!" Carl yelled as the queens galloped away a couple hundred feet then disappeared in a rainbow-colored sparkling mist.

Candy Vargo was still staring at the sky. "Fuck," she muttered.

"What?" I asked.

"Welp, if the Higher Power was pissed that the Four

Horsemen were here, the sky would have gone back to normal when they left."

I looked up. The sky had not gone back to normal. In fact, it looked more threatening. Fuck was correct. "Okay," I said, doing everything in my power to stay calm. "Let's go back inside and figure out the rest of the message. I have a Higher Power to visit."

CHAPTER SEVEN

THE QUEENS WERE GONE, AND I FELT THEIR ABSENCE ACUTELY.
I'd kind of hoped they'd *procure* a home in my sleepy Georgia
town and stay forever. That wasn't going to happen. Crossing
my fingers, I hoped I would see them again. Glancing out of
the window, my stark reality came roaring back.

The sky had grown scarier, and the time to move was now.
I just didn't know how.

Tim pulled out his notebook and started talking. "Now that
we've solved what the significance of three means, I believe we
should tackle the rest."

"I agree," Charlie said as he stood by the window and
watched the sky. "The sooner the better."

When we'd come back in, Charlie had fixed the front door
with a little magic. That was welcome. The temperature had
dropped dramatically. Alana Catherine slept in Jennifer's arms
on the sofa. My human friend dozed right along with her. The
communication with Pandora had clearly exhausted my baby.
The thought of taking her with me to the Higher Power's plane
was not good. My mind raced to figure out a way around it.

I couldn't come up with one.

Candy Vargo paced the room in agitation. Gram, Mr. Jackson, Lura Belle, Dimple and Jolly Sue floated en masse right behind her. Gideon stood as still as a statue next to the fireplace. His expression was unreadable, but his clenched fists at his sides gave his tension away.

"Tim, please read the message," I said, hoping I sounded normal but knowing I probably didn't.

"The game is a riddle. Three must play to win and break the evil spells," Tim read aloud. "The show will go on and the wheels will turn. The answers are questions. The price must be right or the innocent will pay. In the end the choice will be on the strongest. The strongest shall emerge the victor. Anything is possible. You just have to believe. Time is running out."

Closing my eyes, I nodded and let my mind wander. Hell, the first couple of lines sounded like game shows—*Wheel of Fortune*, *Jeopardy* and *The Price is Right*. That was absurd. There had to be deeper meanings. For the life of me, I couldn't think of one. However, it was interesting that the word riddle kept coming up. Steve had said it and then Alana Catherine had communicated it to Pandora.

"Only parts of it makes sense to me," I said, twisting my hair in my fingers. "The time is running out part is pretty freaking clear."

Candy Vargo, chewing on a toothpick, sat down on the floor crisscross applesauce. It was bizarre. She looked up and me and patted the floor next to her. "Wanna join me, asshole?"

"Not really, but I will." I sat down next to the insane woman and waited to see why we were sitting like this. "Speak."

She offered me a toothpick. I took it.

"You speak," she countered. "Get all that shit out of your

head. Can't muddy the waters when you don't know what's lurking beneath."

I took a deep breath and let it rip. "I don't know where I'm going or what to expect. I'm fully aware that I'm supposed to take Gram and Alana Catherine with me. I don't want to. I'd rather go alone. Risking them makes me sick. I'll be worried about protecting them and might screw up the mission. Not to mention, I don't know how to bring them with me. Honestly, what I'd like to do is rip the Higher Power a new asshole, but I'm gonna go out on a limb and say that's probably a bad plan. I'm seriously concerned about Steve, Sam, Sister Catherine, Agnes, Birdie and John. I have no clue what a tear in the Light means, and I have even less of a clue how to fix it. Right now, I'd like to puke."

Candy Vargo flipped me the bird and grinned. "Slow down, mother fucker. First, you're goin' to the Higher Power's plane. You're gonna slow your fuckin' brain down shortly so you can go to sleep and get there."

"What if I go to the wrong place?"

Charlie spoke. "You'll focus on where you wish to be, not where you want to go. Don't think in a linear fashion. Human reasoning rarely works with magic."

"Okay." I nodded. "I'll wish to be where the Higher Power is. Not about a place per se."

"Excellent," he said. "You're getting the hang of this Immortal stuff."

"From your mouth," I muttered with a weak smile.

"Next on the list," Candy said. "You ain't got no choice about who goes. Alana Catherine spoke and we're gonna listen. So, wipe that shit about goin' alone right out of your pea brain. As for how to do it, we'll get to that in a bit. Also, I'd suggest not attacking the Higher Power. It won't fuckin' end well. You feel me?"

"I'd rather not," I replied.

The Keeper of Fate threw her head back and laughed. "You best watch that smart mouth, shitball."

"You're one to talk, turdknocker," I shot right back.

"I ain't the one goin' to the Higher Power," she reminded me.

"Point. Taken," I replied.

"As for the dead that ain't supposed to be here, they'll go back once you've mended the tear." She paused and scratched her head with the toothpick that had been in her mouth. "I don't know what the tear means, and I don't know how to fix it. But remember, nothing is impossible."

"I just have to believe," I said, finishing the phrase that had become our motto.

"That's right, motherfucker," she said, patting me on the head. "You're a badass. Be the badass."

She was correct. I was the badass. People I loved were in danger. I was about to believe more than I'd ever believed. "How will I take Gram and Alana Catherine with me?" I hated the words that left my lips, but time was moving forward and I wasn't. If it was destined to be the past the present and the future, then it would be. I would not screw around with fate. Period.

"Gram can slip inside you as a ghost. Just make sure that you don't mind dive with her. That'll fuck everything up," Candy said.

I sucked my bottom lip into my mouth to keep from telling Candy to fuck off. That would serve no purpose other than getting myself electrocuted by Candy and yelled at by Gram for dropping an F-bomb. I didn't have time for that. "I'd have to hug her with the intention to dive into her mind to make that happen," I told her. "How can Gram slip inside me? Will she get stuck like Pandora did with Cecily?"

As much as I loved Gram, it wasn't an appealing thought to think she might live inside my body for the rest of time.

"I think it'll be just fine, baby girl," Gram said. "Might be a little cold, though."

Cold was an understatement. When a ghost went through a living being it was like being stabbed with icy daggers. The saying 'no pain, no gain' came to mind.

"Gram, I don't mind being cold as long as you're safe," I told her.

"Daisy, you in menopause yet?" Jennifer asked, waking up from her snooze and hearing the tail end of my response to Gram. Jennifer couldn't see or hear the ghosts, but she usually got the gist of the conversation by what everyone else said.

I wanted to remind my buddy that I was only forty and had just given birth, but being rude to Jennifer was not necessary. "I'm not."

"Well balls," Jennifer said. "I was thinking if you got hot flashes, it might counteract the cold. My psychic, Becky, had 'em bad. Poor gal could look right as rain one minute then the next she looked like she'd just taken a shower while fully dressed. Y'all remember Lettie May from the butcher shop?"

Candy Vargo squinted at her. "The nut job who tried to off her husband with a salami?"

"That's the one," Jennifer confirmed. "Lettie May's hot flashes were so terrible that she went into the meat locker to cool down and got locked in there for three days."

"Wait. What?" I asked. "That can't be true. How would no one know she was missing?"

"Her son of a bitch husband locked her in there thinkin'

she'd freeze to death," she explained, much to our horror. "The joke was on him. She loved it! She wasn't sweating, and there was plenty to eat. Although, she did try to off him with a spicy, three-foot-long frozen deli stick when she got out. Concussed the daylights out of that old fool. Lettie May got the butcher shop in the divorce. Renamed it Salami Slammer in honor of her ex doing six years for tryin' to kill her and the beautiful fact she beaned that bastard with a log of meat. She makes a mean summer sausage."

"True that," Candy Vargo agreed.

"Menopause is such an interesting phenomenon," Tim announced, flipping pages of his notebook. "I've studied it so I can be helpful to my friends. Did you know that women not only suffer from hot flashes, mood swing and insomnia, but can gain weight too? Also, menopause can affect your sex life making the vaginal cavity dry and uncomfortable for copulation."

All of the women in the room gave Tim the evil eye—even the dead women. Tim turned bright red and slammed his notebook shut.

"Too much?" he whispered, mortified.

"Way," I said. "Do not ever utter those words in that order in front of a woman again. Ever."

"Good to know, friend," he said.

I shook off Tim's unfortunate overshare and got back on track. "No one ever answered if Gram would get stuck in me."

"Because we don't know," Charlie admitted. "While I don't think so, I can't be definitive in my answer."

That wasn't great at all.

"Should we try it now, Daisy girl?" Gram asked, zipping over to me and hovering in the air by my side.

"Hold that thought," I told her with a smile. I glanced over at Candy. "How will I make sure Alana Catherine is with me?"

"Reaper, you wanna handle this?" Candy Vargo asked.

Gideon closed his eyes for a hot sec then walked over to me and sat down on the ground. "I can bind her to you with a spell."

"Literally?" I asked, confused.

"No, not as in she's glued to you. It just means for the next twenty-four hours she will be where you are."

I took it in and thought about it. "Will it hurt her?"

He shook his head. I could tell he wanted to say more. I had a gut feeling I knew what it was...

"But it will hurt me," I stated.

He nodded. His expression was grim and I could tell he wanted to put some more holes in the plaster. He wasn't happy. "It is painful," he said tightly. "You have the ability to take both your pain and hers."

It was the first time I smiled with relief all day. "That works for me."

"It doesn't sit well with me. Seeing you suffer isn't my idea of a good time," Gideon said flatly. "But it can be done."

"Think about it this way. My pain is our baby's gain."

Gideon cupped my cheek in his hand. "I love you, Counselor."

"I love you more, Reaper," I replied, placing my hand over his.

"Not possible." He raised a brow and kissed my nose.

I wasn't going to fight him. I'd call it a draw. "What about Gram? Can you bind her to me as well?"

He shook his head. "No, she's dead. It only works with those who breathe."

The pain I was about to go through would suck. Hard. But

the icy daggers and whatever agony Gideon's spell would cause would be worth it. No pain, no gain.

I had a lot to gain if this worked and too much to lose if it didn't.

Stealing Cecily's catchphrase, again, I leaned over and kissed the man who made me feel whole. "Let's get this party started."

CHAPTER EIGHT

"Everybody, back the fuck up," Candy Vargo announced.

The Keeper of Fate was glowing orange. It was a crazy look, but I was getting used to it. My normal had become anything but normal. Charlie's eyes were silver. He'd been warned by Candy if he let his power get out of control and made it difficult to breathe, she'd kick his ass so hard he wouldn't sit for a decade. He heeded her warning and tamped it back. Tim was glowing as well. The look was eerie, and I was beginning to wonder how bad this was going to be. It wasn't often that all my friends were lit up at the same time.

The ghosts had been asked to leave the room before the spell took place. There was a chance that it could open a portal and suck the dead into it. That was news to everyone except Gideon. I wanted to inquire as to how he knew it but decided that I didn't want the answer. The gift of keeping Gram, Mr. Jackson, Lura Belle, Dimple and Jolly Sue safe would have to suffice.

"Jennifer," Candy Vargo said, running her hand over the back of her neck. "I'm gonna say you should leave as well."

"Cause I might get sucked up into a portal?" she asked, looking bizarrely excited about the prospect. My buddy watched far too many movies.

"Nope," Candy told her. "Cause what's about to go down ain't nothin' you should see. It's gonna be bloody and gnarly."

"Roger that!" Jennifer hightailed it up the stairs with the dead. She had a hair-trigger gag-reflex, and so did I. If she hurled, I'd hurl. Puking was the last thing I wanted to do right now.

"Where should I be?" I asked Gideon.

My husband had gone full-on Demon. The Grim Reaper's eyes were sparkling blood red, and his ebony-black wings had burst from his back. It was scary and stunning. I found it hot. Getting my head examined was on the to-do list.

"Sit on the couch," he instructed.

Candy delivered Alana Catherine to my open arms. She was now alert and awake. Her little legs were kicking like she was riding a trike, and she was trying to shove her entire fist into her mouth. My gal was talented. It was hard to reconcile that what we were about to do was on the word of the baby trying to eat her hand.

Were we crazy? That was a given.

Had Pandora been playing us? No. I didn't believe she had been. It was all too raw and real. Plus, the message from Alana Catherine made sense to our situation. It was filled with info Pandora couldn't have known. I was still making my peace with what was about to happen.

And then it happened.

Gideon snapped his fingers and produced a wicked-looking, sharp dagger encrusted with shiny red rubies on the handle. The dagger looked ancient. I was sure it was. My daughter and I were the only living people in this room who weren't older than dirt. The weapon was compact and mostly blade. I took a deep breath and willed myself not to gasp. There was no way I was backing out, but I wanted to face it like the badass I believed I was. I'd fought enemies who'd shot fireballs the size of cars and others who'd tried to decapitate me. This was nothing…

"Okay," Gideon said, sounding as tense as I'd ever heard him. "Shortly, I'm going to cast a spell on the knife. When it's done, I'll slice my palm and then yours. We'll clasp hands and mingle our blood. Once that's been accomplished, you will place a drop on Alana Catherine's tongue."

"And?" I asked.

"And that's it," he replied, scrubbing his free hand over his jaw.

I tilted my head in question. "I don't understand how I'll be keeping our daughter from feeling pain."

Gideon was holding on to his composure by a thread. I got it. I really did. He was dealing with the two people he loved most in this world. He was about to inflict what I could only guess was horrific pain. It was killing him. I completely understood. And if the tables were turned, I would do the same. Because, while causing the love of my life severe pain was nearly unimaginable, allowing our daughter to experience it would be even worse.

"You'll hold her close to your body after the blood touches her tongue," he finally said. "As long as she's touching you, you will feel her pain, not her." His lips compressed into a thin, flat line. It was obvious he was at war with himself.

I reached out to him. He took my hand and squeezed it. His bright red eyes were wild and unfocused.

"I love you. I trust you. I believe in you," I said. "You're doing this because you love me and our baby. Here's what I say, let's get this f-ing party started. The faster we go, the faster we come back."

"As you wish," Gideon said, pulling his shit together. He kissed my hand before reluctantly letting it go.

The love of my Immortal life chanted in a language that I'd heard him use before. I didn't understand a word of it. It was haunting and lyrical. If I wasn't anticipating pain, I would have enjoyed it. The blade sparked and hissed. A foggy red mist seeped from it and rolled off like dry ice in hot water. Gideon continued to chant. I was transfixed on his face. His gaze was fixed on mine. I felt his love. I felt the pain of his indecision.

I gave my head the smallest of shakes and then smiled. "We're in this together. No regrets. Just do it."

He nodded and continued. As the chanting stopped, the mist turned to sparkles and burst in the air above the dagger. Alana Catherine squealed and clapped her chubby hands. It seemed as if our baby knew what was happening. I wasn't sure how that was possible, but in our world, pretty much anything seemed possible.

Quickly and almost medically, Gideon ran the blade over his palm and sliced it open. The blood ran down the sides of his hand and dripped to the floor. He stared at the wound for a long moment. There was no time to think. I took the action into my own hands, so to speak. Keeping one arm around our squirming daughter, I shoved my other at him. An offering for his blade.

"Slice my hand," I insisted. "Don't hesitate. You heal quickly, and so do I."

He sliced across my palm with the bloodied dagger. After, we joined hands and held on for dear life.

The word 'pain' didn't even begin to describe the excruci- ating agony that rattled my bones and burned through me like a red-hot poker covered in metal barbs and razor blades. I'd descended into the Darkness with the dead. That little trick was excruciating. I'd fought battles and lost limbs. That had sucked. But this was the worst pain I'd ever experienced.

Screwing my eyes shut and gritting my teeth so I didn't scream, I tried to quench the inferno burning me from the inside out. No avail. My blood was pure molten lava, dehydrating my body as sweat poured off my skin. I held tight to Alana Catherine to keep her from slipping out of my grasp. I used her as a tether to reality, a reminder of why I was holding court for the agony so that I wouldn't let it go. Letting it go meant I couldn't protect my little girl, and I couldn't—no, wouldn't—allow that to happen.

I groaned through gritted teeth as a series of burning jolts rocketed through my body. They started in my stomach and spread fast through the rest of me. I was sure if the pain didn't let up I would black out, but then Gideon wrapped his arms around both me and our baby, giving me the strength I needed to persevere. The pain was intense, but my biggest fear was allowing it to spill over into my child. This was how I kept the bad from touching her. This is how I kept her safe. I held on for what felt like years but had only been a few minutes. Then, suddenly, it ended as quickly as it had begun.

Laughing weakly with intense relief, I peeled part of my soaked shirt away from my body. The sound was gross. My throat was parched and raspy as I uttered, "Water." And "Dry clothes."

"I've got this, fucker," Candy said, waving her hands from across the room and gifting me with new dry clothes and a cold glass of refreshing water.

"Thank you," I whispered, refraining from commenting

that she'd dressed me in mismatched sweats and ratty tennis shoes. I was thankful for a dry outfit.

Gideon held the glass to my lips as I sipped the cool liquid. Miraculously, it quenched me as if chock full of magical electrolytes. Trying to regulate my breathing was harder than expected, but the look of concern on my child's face forced me to have superpowers. Within a few seconds, I no longer sounded like I'd just run a marathon.

Looking down at my palm, I noticed the wound had started to close. There was no way in hell I wanted to go through the first half of what I'd just been through again.

I could do this. I had to. "Round two," I muttered, putting my open palm near my baby's mouth. I glanced up at Gideon who was paler than I'd ever seen him. "Will it break the spell if you help me with the next part?"

He shook his head, reached over and cupped his hand around mine. Gently, he squeezed my palm, and a single drop of our mingled blood landed in Alana Catherine's open mouth. We exchanged a shocked glance. Did she understand her part in this magic? It appeared that she did.

"Babababababababababaaaaaa," she squealed with a giggle.

"Hold her," Gideon insisted. "I'll be here to brace you if it gets to be too much.

My nod was robotic, and I held Alana Catherine close. At her first whimper, I held her tighter.

"Mama's got you," I whispered against the top of her head. "I won't let go. I promise."

The sensations were no less painful than the blood exchange with Gideon, but they were entirely different. Where I'd felt like I was melting from the inside out when Gideon and I had clasped hands, this time I felt as if the literal weight of the world was crushing my lungs and every part of my body.

Speaking was impossible… no matter how much I believed. Trying to breathe through it was not happening either. If it went on much longer, I'd pass out.

Only a fool makes light of agony. Novels glorify it. Movies are made about it. It's not romantic or even noble. It's brutal and cruel. But in this case, it was worth it. Did I want to repeat it? No. Would I do it a million times for my child? Yes.

In the distance, I heard my little girl's happy babbling. It gave me the strength to hold on. She was feeling no pain. That was my reward.

As the pressure began to subside, I was able to take short, shallow gulps of air. Oxygen was glorious. Gideon held both of us as tears streamed down his cheeks. That had to have been horrible to watch. It sucked all kinds of ass to live it.

Again, I hoped this was the one and only time I'd have to do this.

"Are we bound?" I whispered brokenly, looking down at Alana Catherine. She smiled up at me and pointed at my mouth.

"Mamamamamama," she said, touching my chin. "Mama-mamamamama!"

I laughed. She was too young to be speaking. It had to be a mistake, but I was going to pretend that her second word was mama. I needed a win right now.

"You're bonded," Gideon said. His voice was rough, and his eyes were sparking. "I don't ever want to witness that again."

"Trust me," I said with a pained laugh. "I'm with you on that."

"Hate to be a ballbuster," Candy Vargo said, walking over and examining both me and Alana Catherine. "But you got one more fuckin' bout of hell to suffer."

"Fufufufufufufufu," Alana Catherine babbled, waving at a horrified Candy.

"Oh shit," she choked out, glancing around wildly for Gram. "Is that my fault?"

I blew out a raspberry and tried not to laugh. "Yep, that's your fault. You have to tone down the f-bombs or you're going to spend the next year with Gram in the bathroom with a bar of soap in your potty mouth."

Candy Vargo was mortified. I'd never seen that look on her yet. "Baby girl," she cooed at Alana Catherine. "That word is a no-no! Don't be sayin' that crap."

"Nononononononono!" she answered to Candy's relief.

However, when she yelled 'crap' as clear as day, Candy Vargo excused herself from the room and went to get Gram. She was going to be in deep doodoodoodoodoo. However, she was correct. I had one more painful episode to endure before entering the dream state. I had to let Gram into my body. I just hoped I would be able to get her out. Right now, it didn't matter. It was the only way to get the past, present and future to the Higher Power's plane. Even if Gideon could bind me to Gram, I would have declined and let her hop a ride inside me. Once was enough with the binding spell.

"Daisy girl," Gram called out as she zipped down the stairs. "You ain't never gonna believe it!"

There wasn't much I wouldn't believe at this point. "Tell me."

"Daisy!" Jennifer yelled as she ran down the stairs like there was a fire. My dogs, Donna and Karen were on her heels wagging their tails so hard it created a breeze. "Did Gram tell you yet?"

I was confused. We all were. Jennifer couldn't see or hear

the dead. She was human. How in the heck did she know Gram wanted to tell me something?

"Umm…" I didn't know what to say.

"It's nuts!" Jennifer shouted, going right for the wine and drinking it straight from the bottle.

"What's nuts?" Candy Vargo demanded, standing at the bottom of the stairs with a preening Lura Belle, Dimple and Jolly Sue surrounding her. Mr. Jackson was by Gram's side.

"Don't rightly know how it happened," Jennifer said, offering Candy the wine. The Keeper of Fate took a swig and handed it back. "But some kind of weird red mist floated into the guest room where I was hanging out and, all of a sudden, I heard Jolly Sue call me a boil-brained moldwarp! It was hilariously terrifying. At first, I wondered if I was wasted, but I've only had one bottle today. I need at least three to be drunk. And then…"

"I called her a bawdy, crook-plated hussy," Dimple announced with pride. "AND SHE HEARD ME!"

I almost choked on my spit. "Can you still hear them?"

Jennifer nodded, thrilled with the strange turn of events. "I can hear them, but I can't see them."

"That ain't the exciting news, though," Gram said. "Jennifer, tell Daisy what you did for her, you darlin' little gal!"

"Will do, Gram," she said with a belly laugh. "It's a dang good thing I'm goin' through menopause!"

"I am so confused," I muttered.

"Join the club, friend," Tim said with a smile, taking notes on whatever was about to be revealed.

"First things first," Jennifer said. She turned in a full circle. "Am I sparkling?"

"Sparkling?" I asked.

"Like Edward from *Twilight*?" she clarified.

"Umm... no," I told her.

"Damn," she muttered with a laugh. "I was hoping I'd sparkle, but whatever. I have bigger news!"

"For the love of the longest fuckin' lead up I've ever heard, get to it," Candy Vargo grunted.

"Fufufufufufufufufu," Alana Catherine yelled. "Nononononononono!"

Candy Vargo dove behind the couch to avoid Gram's ire.

"Ain't got time to deal with that mess right now," Gram announced. "But when this is done, Candy Vargo you're gonna get your backside tanned. You hear me?"

"Yes, ma'am," she said from under the sofa.

"Can we get back to whatever happened?" Gideon requested.

"Sure thing," Jennifer told him. "Mr. Jackson and I had a nice conversation. Kind of hard to understand him, but once we got goin' it was just fine. Sweet man. I totally approve of him courtin' Gram."

"Yep," I said, getting a little frustrated. She was so excited, I didn't want to rain on her parade, but I had stuff to do and places to go. Not that I wanted to do the stuff or go to the place, but I had to.

"Soooooo," Jennifer said, trying to waggle her eyebrows and failing. Botox was some strong shit. "He and the others explained that Gram has to ride inside you to get to the Higher Power's plane. There was some debate as to if she could leave your body when you guys are done kickin' ass. Well... there's not a debate anymore!"

"Wait. What?" I asked, terrified for my human buddy. "What did you do?"

Gram was turning delighted flips in the air as Mr. Jackson clapped and lost a hand. Dimple, Jolly Sue and Lura Belle flew at me like bombs out of a cannon. They were all talking at once. I caught the words beslubbering hedge pigs and weedy strumpet. The rest sounded like gibberish.

"QUIET!" Charlie bellowed, putting an abrupt stop to the chaos. He walked to the center of the room and silently indicated that everyone should take a seat. Everyone listened. Charlie had that kind of authority. "Jennifer, I'd like you to be more specific, please."

She gave Charlie a thumbs up. He smiled and gave her one right back.

"We tested the theory," Jennifer explained. "Not with Gram, just in case she got stuck in me but with Dimple. That old coot is nuts."

"Thank you, you bat-fouling, clack-dish imbecile," Dimple replied with a wide smile. "It was quite enjoyable. I've never flown directly into a human before."

I didn't want to point out that she'd only been dead for a few days, but Jolly Sue had no problem with it. "Not a big surprise since you've only been deceased for four days, you gorbellied, malt-worm, flax-wench," she told her.

Lura Belle jumped right on in. "Jolly Sue, you can shove it up your mangled, clay-brained clotpole. What Dimple did was heroic!"

"I was worried and suggested we wait for y'all, but Dimple wasn't havin' none of that," Gram said, patting Dimple on the head. "That there old gal had big lady balls!"

"And get this," Jennifer said. "I was in the middle of a hot flash when Dimple dove in and it took it away. I think we could start a business."

"I think not," Gideon said, pressing the bridge of his nose. "It would be quite difficult to explain that a ghost was going to fly through you to cool you down. That's the kind of business that could land you in a psych hold."

Jennifer nodded as she sipped on her wine. "I can see how that might be weird."

Weird was an understatement, but something else piqued my interest. "Didn't it hurt when Dimple flew into you?"

I'd always experienced it as icy daggers stabbing all my internal organs.

"Nope," Jennifer said. "I loved it! But the real kicker was that Dimple was able to come back out."

That was incredibly good news. I wasn't thrilled with the method, but it took some of the weight of what we were about to do off my mind. However, I didn't understand how it had been painless.

I looked over at Dimple. "What was your method? How did you fly into Jennifer?"

Dimple pursed her cat-butt lips in thought for a moment. "I went into her feet and worked my way up. When I got past her intestines, I settled in under her ribcage. I took a three-minute catnap then left the way I entered."

"Wonderful," Lura Belle said, fanning herself. "I'm not fond of intestines—all that lumpish, bugger-mugger mess. I'm quite impressed with your technique, Dimple."

Dimple took a bow. Mr. Jackson applauded and lost his entire arm.

I looked over at Gram. She was grinning like a fool. I grinned right back. "You heard the ancient coot. I say you go for my feet, old lady."

"Can do," Gram said. "Get ready, Daisy girl, I'm a-coming!" Gram flew at my feet then disappeared.

I was shocked into happy silence when I felt no pain. My feeling of gratitude to Jennifer and Dimple was immense. I wasn't sure how much more pain I could take. The fact that Gram hitched a ride without torture on my end was priceless.

"You in there?" I asked.

Her voice was muffled, but we all could hear her. "Sure am! This is just nuts. It's cozy in here. Gotta say, I'm as happy as Karen and Donna layin' on the front porch chewin' on a big ol' catfish head."

I wrinkled my nose. That was gross. Donna and Karen didn't think so, they barked, wagged their tails then took off through the dog door. I was pretty sure there were no catfish laying around, but at the rate the crazy was going, who knew?

"One thing to remember," Tim said. "Time runs differently on different planes. You are bound to Alana Catherine for twenty-four hours as we know time. I'd suggest you work with haste once you arrive at the destination."

I nodded slowly and took that in. Keeping my daughter safe was paramount. I was not going to mess around. "Thank you, Tim."

"Always, friend," he replied with a warm smile.

"Are you ready, Daisy?" Gideon asked, still sounding stressed.

Glancing down at Alana Catherine, I smiled. "You ready, baby?"

"Mamamama," she yelled before she stuck her thumb into her mouth and cuddled close.

"I'm ready too, Daisy girl," Gram shouted from somewhere in my midsection.

"Then I guess it's time to go," I said, reclining back on the couch. "I love everyone in this room. I'm going to do this. I'm going to beat the Higher Power at Its own game."

"Not alone, you're not," Gram added. "That's why you got me and sweet Alana Catherine."

"Not alone," I amended. "And after, I'm coming right back home." I closed my eyes and then opened them, looking straight at my husband. "And when I get back, we're going on our damned honeymoon, come hell or high water. You hear me, Reaper?"

"Loud and clear, Counselor. I'll have you packed and ready," he replied with a sweet kiss to both me and our child. "You will be cautious. You will be smart. And you will come home to me. Period. Nothing else is acceptable."

"Roger that, bossy man," I said with a smile as I realized I was tired.

Going to sleep wasn't going to be a problem.

The rest of the journey? I was about to find out.

CHAPTER NINE

WHERE IN THE HELL WAS I?

I quickly scanned the room, unable to remember where I was or why I'd come.

The overhead lights were fluorescent. The walls were a dull green, and a long plastic-covered beige couch lined one of the walls. It wasn't a large room. In fact, it felt a little claustrophobic. There was one heavy metal door on the far side, and it was closed. No windows. The floor was a faded butter-yellow linoleum that had seen better days. Whoever decorated the room was stuck in the late 1960's.

Wait... was it the 1960's?

For the life of me, I didn't understand anything. What was I doing here? And where exactly was *here*? There was one other woman in the room. She was stunning and about twenty—tons of dark curly hair and unusually beautiful eyes. Oddly, she was wearing an adult-sized pink onesie that should have been on a baby, not a full-grown woman. I felt like I knew her, but couldn't place her. She gave me a shy smile and a wave. I waved back. When I was about to inquire who she was, something insane occurred.

"Daisy?" a vaguely familiar voice called out. "Can I come out?"

I glanced down at my stomach in terror. Had I eaten someone? Was I high? Was I in the waiting room of a mental institution? Why in the hell was I wearing mismatched sweats and crappy tennis shoes? Nothing made sense.

"Did you hear that?" I whispered to the fashion-impaired gal... not that I looked much better.

"I did," she replied with a sweet smile. "I think you should let her out."

"How?" I asked, wondering if she was as crazy as I appeared to be.

She shrugged. "Tell her it's okay to come out now."

Made sense. "Umm... sure. Come on out."

Much to my shock, a full-grown old woman flew out of my feet. I screamed. I didn't remember smoking any pot or taking hallucinogenic drugs, but I must have. Not much else could explain a woman exiting my body through my feet. I didn't think I even liked drugs, but there was a first time for everything. Backing myself up against the wall, I wondered if I could make a run for the door and escape. Although, the old lady didn't seem dangerous, nor did the pretty woman in the onesie. They were both adorable and the old one was very talkative.

"Well, butter my butt and call me a biscuit," she said, looking down at her dress. "This right here is the dress I got buried in. I think I'm lookin' spiffy!" She stared at her hands in delight. "I can't see through them no more! Feel kinda like Pinocchio! I'm a real old lady again with skin and age spots. That just dills my pickle."

This was definitely a mental institution. She was nuts. There was a distinct possibility all three of us were off our rockers.

Deciding to jump in with an icebreaker, I got right to the point. "Hi, I'm Daisy." At least I could remember my name. That was something. "I'm not sure where I am right now. Do either of you nice ladies happen to know?"

The look they exchanged was filled with horror. My stomach cramped. Something was very wrong.

"Who am I?" the old lady demanded.

"Is that a trick question?" I asked warily.

"Nope," she said, crossing her skinny arms over her chest and giving me the eyeball. The move was familiar. "You seem to be as confused as a fart in a fan factory. You know who I am, Daisy girl."

I shook my head. I didn't know who she was. I had a feeling I was supposed to, but I didn't. Looking over to the onesie girl, I smiled apologetically. "Am I supposed to know you too?"

Her smile went right to my heart and made me feel strangely whole. "Yes, but I look very different from the last time you saw me."

The old gal in her burial dress was getting perturbed. "You think she banged her noggin on the trip?" she asked, Onesie.

"I don't," she said. "There's some kind of spell in this room. Some kind of trap is my guess."

I looked around. What was the girl talking about? A spell? I blew out a long slow breath and tried to think of a plan. I expected men in white coats to show up with straightjackets at any moment.

"I'm out of here," I announced, walking over to the door and trying to open it. Of course, it was locked. If this were a horror movie, the door would be locked right before everyone died violently.

The pretty young girl walked over and extended her hand. I could remember a handsome man telling me to be cautious. Was I supposed to be cautious of the girl? That didn't sit right. I felt a strong pull to both of the women. Very strong.

Slowly, I took her hand, and part of the fog in my brain cleared. I did know these women, but I still wasn't sure why or how.

"Three is a powerful number," she said, glancing over at the old woman and extending her other hand. "The past, the present and the future need to come together. The game is a riddle. Three must play to win and break the evil spells."

"I know those words," I whispered, doing my best to recall why.

"I know you do," the girl said, gently squeezing my hand.

Her touch was magical and I never wanted to let go.

"Gram, please join us," she said.

The woman she called Gram hustled over, took Onesies' hand in hers, then extended the other to me. "Daisy girl, hold my hand. Let's break this dang spell."

I was beginning to think she wasn't insane, and neither was Onesie. Maybe I was the only one who had lost her marbles. Tentatively, I took the old gal's hand in mine. My entire body tingled as the rest of the fog dissipated. The shock of the truth hit me like a cement block thrown at my head from close range. My knees buckled, and I dropped to the floor with a thud. Onesie was my baby girl who wasn't a baby anymore except for the unfortunate outfit she was wearing. Alana Catherine was all grown up and saving me when I should be the one protecting her. Gram was the woman who'd loved me and raised me. She was dead, but here she wasn't. Gram was wearing the dress I'd chosen for her at her funeral. She looked gorgeous and very much alive. I was wearing shitty sweats and ugly tennis shoes because that was what Candy Vargo, the OG of badasses, had dressed me in after the binding spell to protect my daughter.

We were on the Higher Power's plane of existence and locked in a room that had been spelled. Thankfully, the spell had only affected me. If it had dinged all three of us, we'd be screwed. My desire to beat the Higher Power's ass intensified. But seeing Alana Catherine and Gram kickstarted my protection instinct into high gear.

I was in it to win it. We'd somehow passed the first test no thanks to me, but that was the power of three.

The tears came unbidden and there was nothing I could do to stop them. My grandmother and daughter joined me on the floor in the cryfest. We held tight to each other and didn't let go.

"We have to move now, girlies," Gram said. "Tim told us that we can't mess around."

I squeezed both of them tighter. "What if I forget again?"

Alana Catherine touched my cheek. Immediately, I place my hand over hers. "If you do... if any of us do, we know how to beat it. We stick together and figure it out."

I squinted at my lovely and wise daughter. "Do you understand why we're here?"

She laughed. It remined me of delicate chimes. "Strangely, yes."

"All of it?" I pressed, making sure I didn't need to explain anything to her. Knowledge was power, and we needed all that we could get.

"All of it," she assured me.

"How?" I was confused.

She shrugged. "Magic works in mysterious ways, Mom."

I sucked my bottom lip into my mouth to keep from crying. I failed. "You called me mom," I blubbered.

"Umm… that's because you're my mom," she replied with a raised brow that was so reminiscent of Gideon it made me gasp.

"You look like your dad," I told her, unable to stop staring at the grownup version of my child.

"Sperm has an interesting way of making that happen," she replied with a naughty wink.

I was no longer crying. Instead, I laughed.

"She's a spicy little thing," Gram said with a grin. "Just like me!"

"And me," I added. "One more question."

"Ask," Alana Catherine said.

"When we go back, will you be a baby again?"

My daughter was perplexed for a beat. "I'm not sure. Will it bother you if I'm not?"

"Hell to the no," I said quickly. "You could come back as a skunk and I'd love you to the end of time."

"Lordy have mercy," Gram choked out. "Don't say things like that, baby girl. Words have power. Don't you be forgettin' that!"

Gram was right and I hoped hard that I hadn't just accidently doomed my child for life. Heck, if I'd screwed up and turned my baby into a skunk, I'd have Gideon do some of his voodoo so I could take her place and she could live an odor-free life. Deciphering what-ifs was a waste of time and time was not a luxury that we had.

"Moving on," I said, looking at how we were dressed. We were a hot mess other than Gram. "We look really bad."

"You think?" Alana Catherine commented. "I'm wearing a onesie."

"You looked cute in it this morning," I pointed out.

"That was then, this is now," she shot right back with a grin.

Without any fanfare or warning, she wiggled her nose and did her own version of voodoo.

"Wouldja look at that?" Gram gasped.

The three of us were now sporting black from head to toe —black pants, long-sleeved fitted black shirts and fabulous black combat boots.

"I figured we should look the part," Alana Catherine said.

"Of?" I questioned, loving her choice.

"Badass Death Counselors," she replied, pulling both Gram and me to our feet.

"The past, the present and the future," I said with a nod of approval. "I say we go fix the tear in the Light and get back home."

"How we gonna do that, Daisy child?" Gram asked.

"Only one way to find out," I said, waving my hand and disintegrating the door to dust.

CHAPTER TEN

WE WALKED OUT OF THE 1960's AND RIGHT INTO THE 1980's.

"Well, I'll be damned," Gram whispered in awe as we walked onto the empty set of a TV game show. The studio was cavernous. There was a lit-up stage and bleachers for the audience. Everything was clean, shiny and psychedelically colorful. It felt incredibly ominous.

This wasn't just any game show, it was *Wheel of Fortune*... or a bastardized version of it. A large spinning-wheel was on a platform stage, and the wheel was divided into multiple segments. Behind the wheel, a massive puzzle board composed of rectangular tiles, that, if this farce followed the actual game, would light up when correct guesses were made and the tiles were turned.

"The show will go on, and the wheels will turn," Alana Catherine said, repeating what she'd communicated earlier through Pandora.

"Do you recall saying all of that?" I asked her.

She nodded. "I do. It's fuzzy, but I do."

"Do you know what it means?" I questioned, hoping she could get us ahead of the game, so to speak.

"I wish I did, but I don't. I'm sorry."

"Ain't nothin' to be sorry for," Gram told her, taking the words out of my mouth. "Your mama's a badass, just like you and me. She's just looking for all the angles. We're from deep in the south, where sushi's called bait. We don't leave no stone unturned."

Amid a bad situation where things could get ugly fast, Gram made me smile. The woman always knew how to make me smile, and she always would.

"Do you think we're the contestants or the audience?" my daughter asked as we crossed the sound stage and approached the wheel.

"Not sure," I said. "But Steve said to start with the ending I desire and work my way back."

"You got any idea how to do that, Daisy girl?" Gram asked.

"None whatsoever," I replied. "The ending is sending the dead back into the fully functional Light. This game must be how we work our way back." I sounded ridiculous to my own ears, but we had to start somewhere. Situations in our world rarely happened without reason. There had to be a reason for this...

I stopped dead in my tracks when we got to the wheel. The Higher Power was not just playing games, It was playing hardball. My fists clenched at my sides, but I made sure to keep my body language calm. Even though it seemed like it, I didn't believe we were alone on this set. It was watching.

The wheel was similar in size to the one on the TV show. However, what was on the triangles made my stomach turn. Instead of dollar amounts, there were names. Names of people

I knew. Names of people I cared for. Except for the two black and white bankrupt signs, the names Sam, John and Birdie repeated all over the wheel. They'd been three of the six ghosts standing on my porch who should have been in the Light. I'd helped them go into the Light. Were we about to play for their lives?

"This is fucked," I said flatly.

"I'm gonna give you a pass on that F-bomb since I agree, darlin'," Gram said. "In fact, I'm gonna give all of us an F-bomb pass during this entire mission."

I glanced over at her. "Candy Vargo will crap her ugly sweatpants when she finds out."

Gram giggled. "That sweet gal will get over it."

Sweet was kind of a stretch when describing the Keeper of Fate, but Gram loved her. I loved her, too, but to me, she was more salty than sweet.

I looked back at the names on the wheel and my mind raced with memories.

Birdie was a trip—real name, Ethel. I called her Birdie because her mission in death was to flip me off as much as possible. As a ghost, Birdie enjoyed stashing random body parts all over the house to freak me out. That went over like a lead balloon. However, she was truly silly, and I adored her.

Back when she was squatting in my home, I was positive the ghost had been calling me a hooker. Turned out that she'd been a lady of the evening during her life. She'd passed away from a heart attack after blowing a famous politician. Birdie had clarified that she'd been a very high-paid escort and enjoyed her job. I'd enjoyed being around her. She was all kinds of wonderfully wrong. However, what she had done after she'd died made me love her even more.

My mother, Alana, had been Birdie's Death Counselor. Clarissa, the Angel of Mercy before me, had it out for my mom. Wanted her dead and she'd succeeded. However, Birdie was a hooker with a heart of gold. In thanks to my mother for vindicating her after death, Birdie stole my mom's soul from the vile Clarissa and brought her to my BFF Missy's great-grandmother. Missy's granny, like Missy, was a Soul Keeper. Missy's granny kept my mother's soul inside her for safe-keeping and, unbeknownst to Missy, had passed the soul to her great-granddaughter right before she died. Missy had kept my mom and Birdie protected from Clarissa for decades. The reason souls came to me was that they had unfinished business. Birdie's unfinished business was to let me know where my mom's soul was hidden. It was one of the greatest gifts I'd ever been given.

My lovely bird-flipping buddy had gone into the Light once her message had been delivered. I would owe her until the end of time. Birdie was one of the many beautiful reasons I would repair the rift in the Light.

My eyes moved to the next name—John.

John Dunn, age fifty at death. Banker. Wealthy. His death had been ruled a suicide. It was not a suicide. It was murder. John had been a lovely and level-headed man in both life and death. He'd also had shitty taste in women. He'd been murdered by his much younger wife, Sarina. She was a diabolical woman who'd been after his life insurance payout and all of his assets. John's unfinished business was getting me to rescue his black lab, Karen, from the pound where his wife had taken the dog after his death and to prove that he hadn't killed himself.

The Karen part of the mission had been easy. I'd adopted her and loved her with all my heart. I couldn't replace John, but I could give her a spectacular life. John had been pleased about that. Proving Sarina had killed him was more complicated. Since all of the proof was coming from a dead guy, against my better judgement, I'd gotten my lawyer sister Heather involved. Color me shocked as all get out when it was revealed she wasn't exactly human. The revelation had started a chain of events, exposing that many of the people in my life were not who I thought they had been. But that wasn't part of John's story. It was part of mine.

Heather had been a bulldog and destroyed Serina Dunn in a court of law. With Serina facing life in prison and Karen having a loving home, John no longer had any unfinished business. He'd tried to give me all of his money. It was a lot of money, but I'd said no. After a little illegal tampering by Heather and me with his will, John's fortune went to the Humane Society at his request. He'd left this plane vindicated and at peace. I was proud I'd helped get him justice. It had been my true pleasure.

The fact that his name and life had been reduced to a cardboard triangle on a wheel made me sick.

My eyes moved one space over and landed on Sam's name. My heart beat hard and fast in my chest. I thought about the old man often. Sam had been the first ghost I'd helped, and he held a very special place in my heart. When the ghosts first showed up, I thought I was having a psychotic break—thought I'd lost my damned mind.

I hadn't. It had been real.

Sam's sweet and loving persistence taught me how to be the Death Counselor before I even understood what a Death Counselor was. Sam had been in his eighties when he died of a heart attack. He was one of the most adorable little old men I'd ever had the pleasure of meeting. I'd wanted to keep him and make him my grandpa, but that wasn't how it worked. Sam's unfinished business had to do with his wife, Addie. She was in the early stages of dementia and would often lose her glasses. The night he died, he'd noticed she'd put them in the cookie jar again. He was beside himself that she wouldn't know where they were since he was no longer there to find them for her. The heartbreaking kicker was that her wedding ring was on the chain. Her arthritis had gnarled her hands a bit, and she wore her beloved piece of jewelry on her glasses chain.

Sam convinced me that true love existed and that I should commit my first breaking-and-entering. I smiled at the memory.

Sam's home had been lovely. It was an older modest Craftsman with a nicely landscaped yard. Thankfully, it was the last house at the end of a tree-lined street and there were no streetlights.

"Are you seeing this?" Gram asked. "It's like it's my memory, only it ain't mine."

"It's Mom's," Alana Catherine said. "She's showing us."

"Am I?" I asked. Why was I reliving the night I'd helped Sam move on into the light? I wasn't sure why this was happening now, but it had to be important, right? Or maybe it was the Higher Power trying to distract us from the game.

"Don't fight it," Alana Catherine stated, her tone so adult and wise beyond her few months.

I nodded absently as the memory overtook all my senses and threw me into the past. *"I'm going to park a few houses down and we'll walk,"* I told Sam, *who'd grunted his assent. "If we get busted on the street, I'll pretend like we're just out for an early morning run... or that I'm out for a run. Don't think anyone will notice you, Sam. No offense."*

Sam giggled... kind of. His frail little frame trembled with excitement. I felt insanely great with all the stress on the word insane. It was crazy what I was about to do, but it was already established that I'd lost my mind.

"Is there a key hidden anywhere?" I asked, hoping to God there was.

I began to add up all the things that could go wrong. A security system was at the top of the list. I also didn't want to break a window that Sam's wife would have to pay to get repaired. If she was living on a fixed income, which I assumed she was, she didn't need the expense of replacing a window.

Sam nodded and pointed at the welcome mat on the front porch as we quietly approached the house.

Quickly grabbing the key, I stayed low and made my way around the house. My heart had been beating so loud I was sure it would wake up the dead.

Shaking my head, I grinned. I'd already woken up the dead—a whole hell of a lot of them.

"Sam, do you have a dog?" I asked, stopping my forward motion and regretting I hadn't put a few dog treats into the pocket of my all-black break-in attire.

"Naawwwooo," he grunted softly.

Heaving a sigh of relief, I bellycrawled the rest of the way to the back door. I would be filthy when I got home, but I figured this was the way to do it. Of course, I had no clue how to do it, but I planned to fake it till I made it on this one.

"Is the cookie jar in the kitchen?" I asked, slowly rising and peeking through the windowpane on the back door. Thankfully, the light over the sink was on and illuminated the countertop. "Is that it on the counter?"

Sam nodded. Maybe this would be easier than I'd originally thought. Open the door. Grab the glasses. Put them on the counter by the teapot and haul ass out. What could go wrong?

So much. So much could go wrong.

"Let's do this," I whispered to Sam—and then froze.

My dear dead buddy was crying... or trying to. It was heart-breaking and my stomach clenched. Had I done the right thing? Was this too painful for Sam?

Shit.

"Sam," I said, reaching out to touch his withered, semi-transparent cheek. "If you don't want to go through with this, we can leave now."

"Waauufff lassssh gaussaus," he said through his anguish. "Fiiauxxx."

Breathing in and exhaling slowly, I nodded. "I'll fix this for you. I promise. Stay here."

Sam nodded and blew me a kiss. It made an unappealing squishy sound and I almost gagged. However, it was the thought and the love behind the gesture that enabled me to smile at him.

My hands fumbled clumsily as I pushed the key into the lock and prayed hard that there wasn't an alarm about to go off. I had no clue who I was praying to since I didn't really believe, but it felt like a good thing to do. My head felt woozy and my mouth went dry. While everything around me seemed like real time, my movements felt like I was under water.

I was not cut out for a life of crime. If I wasn't doing something good, I'd be out of here so fast Sam's barely attached head would spin. Anxiety gripped me and my feet turned into lead weights. If Sam wasn't smiling at me so hopefully, I would have turned and ran.

"Here goes nothing," I whispered as I tiptoed across the kitchen.

The kitchen was warm and inviting—all done in blue and white and immaculate. It smelled like lemon cleaner and cookies. I felt immediate comfort and terror at the same time. Breaking and entering didn't include admiring décor. I was sure of that.

The glasses were right where I'd seen them in Sam's mind earlier and, thankfully, so was the teapot. Quickly and silently, I put the glasses with the chain holding the wedding ring next to the teapot. Not hard at all. However, I almost puked when I replaced the cookie jar lid and made a loud noise. I wasn't very good at this. I was far more skilled at gluing dead people's appendages back on. I knew I couldn't be good at everything, but a little stealth would have come in handy right now.

"Crap," I hissed as I heard a movement from upstairs.

Swiftly looking around to make sure I had completed the bizarre mission, I hightailed it back out of the door and locked it with the key.

"Come on, Sam," I said as I hit the ground and began to belly-crawl back around the house.

Sam didn't move. His partial nose was pressed to the glass and he waited.

Damn it, what was I supposed to do now? Did I leave him? Would he be able to find his way back to my house? Was I being ridiculous? Yes. He'd found my house once. He could find it again. However, his sense of direction sucked and it could take him days to find me.

I did the only thing I could do. I did the crazy-stupid thing. Why? Because Sam meant something to me. I loved him and I was batshit nuts. I bellycrawled back to where he stood... or floated, to be more accurate.

"We have to leave," I whispered as I peeked into the kitchen.

Sam said nothing. He placed his decomposing hand in mine and gently squeezed.

He wanted to see his wife find her glasses. I understood. However, there was a slight problem here. She couldn't see him, but she could definitely see me.

Moving my head to the right of the door, I peeked into the bottom corner of the glass with one eye. It was still dark out. I had dark hair and was dressed all in black. Plus, she wouldn't be wearing her glasses. It was risky, but if I was being honest, I would love to see her *find her ring and glasses too. If I was going to partake in illegal activities, I should get to reap the reward of a misdemeanor well done... or something like that.*

The little old woman entered the kitchen and turned on the overhead light. She was in her bathrobe and slippers. She was positively adorable. Sam sighed next to me in happiness and anticipation.

She glanced around the kitchen in confusion. I ducked down so she wouldn't see me and then curiosity got the best of me. Slowly I rose up and peeked again.

She gasped and placed both of her hands over her heart. Her body began to shake with sobs as she carefully walked to the teapot and touched her wedding ring with such reverence that my eyes filled with tears. Sam's body trembled beside me. I couldn't look at him or I would truly lose it. I just held tight to his hand and watched.

Taking the glasses with the ring attached into her gnarled hands, she kissed her ring and began to laugh.

I couldn't hear a word she said, but her intention was clear. Pointing at the ceiling, she shook her finger and laughed through her tears. As her lips continued to move, I could make out the words Sam and I love you.

Glancing over at Sam, I gasped and almost cried out. My chest felt tight and my head began to throb.

Gently pulling me to the side of the house, Sam smiled and touched my cheek.

He was no longer a decaying corpse of a man. However, he was still dead. An ethereal and somewhat blinding golden glow surrounded my friend, and his body was restored to what it must have been before he'd passed. He was beautiful. Sam's eyes twinkled and his smile would stay etched in my memories always.

"Sam?" I whispered in a panic, not understanding what was happening.

"Thank you, Daisy," he said in the voice that was the same one I recognized from being inside his mind earlier. "I can go now."

As he began to fade away, my tears came quickly. I knew this was the last time I would ever see Sam. He'd stayed to make sure his beloved found what she treasured the most. He was moving on. Selfishly, I didn't want him to go. In the short time I'd had the privilege of knowing him, I'd grown to love him. This was the suckiest, most beautiful experience I'd ever had.

"Bye, Sam," I whispered, reaching out to touch the golden glow surrounding his diminishing body.

It was warm and inviting—felt like silky liquid. I waited for Sam to completely disappear before I got back on my stomach and began to crawl. My heart was shattered, but it also felt strangely full. I'd just helped my friend move on. It was clear to me he was going somewhere lovely. The golden glow was a sure sign.

I blinked as the memory faded and the *Wheel of Fortune* stage reappeared.

Gram was sniffling. "That was just beautiful, Daisy girl."

"I agree," I told her, still unsure why I'd relived the memory.

"It was your first time," Alana Catherine said.

"Yeah, I know." I shook my head. "I'd managed to help Sam's wife, and that had put Sam on track to cross over."

My daughter smiled gently. "That's not what I mean."

"Then what?" It couldn't be the breaking-and-entering part. "My first time being a criminal?"

She shook her head and chuckled. "No, Mom."

My heart zinged at hearing her call me mom again. I thought it was something I would never grow tired of. "My head's a little fuzzy, daughter. Why don't you spell it out for me?"

She laughed now, and the sound was magical. "It was the first time you learned that anything was possible as long as you believed. Sam helped teach you that lesson, and it's one you need to hold onto."

There it was again. Belief. I gave my daughter an incredulous stare. "You're going to make a great Immortal." When her brow arched, I added, "You already know how to talk around a topic in a way that still makes me feel clueless."

"You got this, girlie," Gram encouraged. "Time to play this game and whoop some butt, so your hard work with them ghosties don't get undone."

Sighing, I touched the names on the wheel. "They're going back into the Light where they belong." I ran my hands through my hair and cased the room. No one was visible but us. I still didn't believe we were alone. "I just need to figure out how to do it."

"You don't have to figure it out alone," Alana Catherine said.

"That's right!" Gram added. "We're the Father, Son and Holy Ghost. Ain't no one that can beat that."

I wanted to point out that she was nuts, but the army of skunks that entered the stage shocked me to silence. They were armed with tiny grenades and razor-sharp swords. It was not right.

They were scared, angry and unbelievably cute. I had a thing for small furry creatures. Not that skunks were like dogs or even cats, but they were cute. Of course, the fact that they were armed was alarming...

"Am I wrong or are they kind of adorable?" Alana Catherine whispered.

"Like mother, like daughter," I said with a wince. "Yes, they're cute, but they also look deadly."

"No sudden movements," Gram whispered, horrified by the sight. "They blow butt bombs when they're startled."

"Umm… Mom," Alana Catherine said.

"What?"

"You have a fertile imagination," she stated flatly. "You might want to keep that in check."

I closed my eyes. This was my fault. Bringing up skunks was going to bite us in the ass or worse.

CHAPTER ELEVEN

THE SKUNKS DIDN'T SEEM FRIENDLY. THERE WERE ABOUT FIFTY of them, and they'd spread themselves out around the large room. Most of them sat in the bleachers. They watched us with narrowed eyes and their little paws on their grenades. I couldn't believe any of it. It was like a fever dream or a really bad comedy-horror movie. But this wasn't a movie, and it definitely wasn't a comedy. Cute or not, I'd end their smelly asses if they came at us.

I'd dealt with lots of deadly enemies in my short time as an Immortal. However, none of them were as sweet looking as the furballs sitting in the audience. How was this even happening?

"Do you think them little stinkers understand English?" Gram asked, barely moving her lips.

"Are you being for real?" I asked.

"Totally," she said. "I ain't never seen a skunk with a dang grenade before and they're sittin' like people for the love of everything strange. Didn't think a skunk needed a weapon since their butts are weapons that smell bad enough to gag a maggot."

Gram's way with words never disappointed. And she was correct about them sitting like they were human. More than half had their little furry legs crossed. A couple even sat criss-cross applesauce. It upped the adorable factor substantially. "Umm... I guess since this is from my unfortunate imagination that the skunks understand English."

"That's good," she grunted.

"Why is that good, old lady?" I asked.

Gram leaned into Alana Catherine and me. With a lowered voice, she explained her plan. "Welp, it's a well-known fact from the Animal Channel that skunks can be friendly and playful. Love me some Animal Channel. When I ain't watching a game show, I love them sweeter than sugar rescue stories. So, what I'm sayin' is that skunks ain't all that bad. I mean aside from the knives, grenades and the resting bitch faces, they're sorta irresistible."

"They're legal to own as pets in seventeen states," Alana Catherine added.

I squinted at my child in disbelief. "How in the world do you know that? You were a baby this morning."

She grinned and shrugged. "I'm with Aunt Jennifer a lot, and that woman knows a lot of insane facts."

"Truth," I muttered. Jennifer was the queen of weird and inappropriate trivia. Still, I hadn't realized my baby's brain had absorbed what she'd heard. Trying to make sense out of the senseless was a waste of time. I just went with it. "Okay, so skunks are playful and friendly and can be kept for pets."

"In seventeen states," my daughter repeated with a wink and a grin.

"Right. So, with that being said, why do you want to know if they speak English?" I asked Gram.

"Hear me out," she said. "I know me some game show etiquette since I'm addicted to 'em. Before every show, they have a warm-up act to get the audience into the spirit. It's usually a comedian. I think them skunks are the audience, and I need to get them into the spirit so those stinkers don't turn on us. Gotta wipe them resting bitch faces off them furry critters and turn their frowns upside down. Get 'em on our team so they don't blow us up or aim a stinky at us that singes the hair right off our heads."

"I think that might be one of the weirdest things you've ever said," I told her.

"Weirder than when I told Verna Lee Smith that her pants were so tight, I could see her religion?" Gram questioned.

Alana Catherine tried not to laugh.

My daughter failed. So did I. Gram was a firecracker. She was also seriously funny.

Shaking my head, I covertly scanned the crowd of skunks. They did seem to be the audience. I wondered which one of them was the Higher Power... if any. A horrible thought occurred to me. Were we even on the freaking Higher Power's plane?

"We're in the right place," Alana Catherine promised.

Again, I was in disbelief. "Did you just read my mind?"

She smiled. "Nope. Your face. And this is the right plane. I feel it in my gut. It feels familiar."

Her statement was weirder than Gram's about Verna Lee Smith's privates, but I'd have her explain later when we weren't surrounded by armed and dangerous skunks.

Trying not to think too hard so I didn't come up with a myriad of reasons why Gram shouldn't be the warm-up act, I followed my gut. "Go for it, Gram."

And she did.

"Howdy! Howdy! How we doin' on this fine day?" she called out waving at the skunks.

Not one skunk made a sound. If anything, they looked more furious.

"Tough crowd," Gram said with a chuckle. "No worries. Gram is here to tickle your funny bone and put a metaphorical cork in your butts!"

Again, silence. I was stunned to silence as well. I wasn't sure how threatening them with what basically amounted to a butt plug shoved up their rear ends was going to win them over. That didn't deter Gram. She was one determined gal.

"Lemme tell you somethin', ladies and gents," she said in her outdoor voice. "Hungry coyotes are like hemorrhoids. Pain in the tushy when they come down through the cracks in the hill and always a relief when they go back up the mountain."

That got a few laughs and a few groans. At least none of them lobbed a grenade at us. It was somewhat of a comfort to know we could get killed on this plane but not die. However, that meant whatever we killed would also come back.

"Try this one on for size," Gram said, getting into her groove. She'd grabbed a broom lying on the floor and used it as a microphone. "What do you get if you cross a skunk and an elephant?"

No one answered.

"Come on now," she said. "Ain't y'all Stinky Petes got a guess?"

The skunks exchanged glances then one raised a paw. I heaved a sigh of relief that there wasn't a grenade in it.

"You! Over there," Gram yelled with excitement. "Gimme your best guess, Pepé Le Pew."

The skunk's voice was high and squeaky. I had no clue if it

was male or female. They all looked exactly the same. "The answer is, I don't know but you can smell it from miles away."

"Bingo, Polecat!" Gram shouted.

The crowd chuckled. A few of the skunks put down their grenades and swords to high-five the one who'd provided the answer to the joke.

"Another," a skunk yelled.

"On it," Gram assured her fan. "What's black and white and green?"

The audience leaned forward in anticipation of the answer.

Gram didn't leave them hanging. "Two skunks fightin' over a pickle!"

That one got belly laughs. The entire situation was bizarre, but Gram was handling it like a pro. I never would have thought to tell armed-to-the-teeth skunks jokes.

"That's why all three of us need to be here," Alana Catherine said.

"My face?" I questioned.

"Your face," she confirmed.

There was more to it than that. I was connected to my child on a very deep level. It wasn't explainable, but it didn't need to be explained. It was what it was and it was beautiful.

"Alrightyroo," Gram said, doing a little jazz square and getting whoops and yee-haws from the crowd. "What happened when the skunk wrote a book?"

"Don't know," a squeaky voice called out.

Gram dropped her broom and slapped her hands onto her hips. "Well, I do! It became a best-smeller!"

The clapping was loud. The laughs were louder. Gram had them eating out of her hand. "And to finish up my set, I got one more for ya!"

The audience cheered. Not a single skunk was armed

anymore. The weapons had been neatly placed under their chairs. So far, so good.

Alana Catherine whispered in my ear. "Spiritually, skunks symbolize fearlessness, protection and balance. The black and white of their fur embodies the balance between the dark and the light."

"Dude, daughter," I said with an amazed laugh. "I hate to be a broken record, but how do you know that? That doesn't sound like Jennifer trivia."

She grinned and shook her head. "Honestly, I'm not sure. Maybe Tim? But, really, I don't have a clue. The answers just keep coming to me. It's kind of handy, though. Right?"

"Right," I agreed, giving her a quick hug and a kiss on the cheek.

"One more thing," she said with a scheming expression on her gorgeous face.

I stared at her. I couldn't read her mind, but I had a very good idea of what she was about to say.

"You want a pet skunk," I stated with a mini eye roll.

She laughed. "I want a pet skunk."

"You're gonna have to ask your dad about that," I replied, avoiding the issue with what I thought was finesse.

"Pretty sure dad is wrapped around my finger," she pointed out.

This time I laughed. "Pretty sure you're correct."

My girl was a sly one. But... I wouldn't mind a pet skunk either as long as it didn't have a stinker, grenades or a sword.

Gram hustled back over with a self-satisfied smirk. "Restin' bitch faces are gone! I right like them little critters. Wouldn't mind having a skunk as a pet."

Alana looked at me with a raised brow.

"Crazy runs in the family," I muttered.

"Five minutes until show time," a harried woman yelled, running onto the stage with a clipboard in her hand.

The lights on the stage grew brighter and made me squint. Canned elevator music came from invisible speakers hidden in the walls, and a large camera on a tripod appeared from out of nowhere and landed at the edge of the stage.

The woman running around was a hot mess. Tall but hunched over. Most of her hair had escaped her ponytail and hung in her face. Her headset held some of it back, but most of her face was obscured. Her jeans were frayed, and her t-shirt was half tucked.

"Bad juju," Gram whispered.

I didn't get that feeling, but I wasn't second-guessing the woman who'd raised me. "You think she's the Higher Power?" I asked so softly Gram and Alana Catherine had to lean in to hear me.

"Don't know," Gram said.

"No," Alana Catherine said firmly at the same time.

Whatever she was, she seemed to be in charge. She eyed us with exasperation. "You couldn't have worn something more colorful?" she snapped. "Black doesn't look great on film. It's a game show, not a funeral."

"We didn't know we were going to be on a game show," I explained in a polite tone. I was sure pissing anyone off here wouldn't go over well.

"Well, you are," she huffed. "Get into places and be prepared to look like shit on TV."

She stomped away and hissed at the skunks. They immediately picked up their weapons and hissed back.

"You think Pat Sajak and Vanna White are here?" Gram asked, trying to sound casual, but not quite making it.

135

"Doubtful," I said just as the people in question walked out onto the stage and made me a liar.

"Holy heck!" Gram squealed. "I think I've died and gone to Heaven!"

"One, Heaven is more of a concept than a place," I told her. "Two, let's not talk about dying. You saw what happened after I mentioned skunks."

"True that, Daisy girl," Gram said, looking sheepish. "Just got excited that Pat and Vanna are here."

"Not sure that's actually Pat and Vanna," Alana Catherine said quietly.

My girl was spot on. The real Pat and Vanna were classy and dignified. The fake Pat and Vanna were not. My mouth hung open in a perfect O as the duo twerked like they were on fire then slapped each other's rear ends like they were putting out a fire. The sound echoed through the cavernous room and was embarrassing to watch. Even the skunks had covered their eyes with their grenades. I sent a quick wish out into the Universe that none of the little stinkers blew themselves up by accident.

"Are we ready to play... *Wheel. Of. Fortune?*" Fake Pat Sajak demanded, leering at Fake Vanna White.

"You bet your blue balls we are," Vanna squealed, disrobing down to her bra and spanks. She marched over to the big letterboard and flipped off the audience. Pat laughed like a loon.

"Oh, my heck," Gram said, fanning herself. "I'm shocked Vanna wears spanks. Thought she was all natural."

"It might look like her, but that's not Vanna," I ground out under my breath. "And that's definitely not Pat."

Pat brought my theory home by humping the edge of the

wheel and faking a massive orgasm. At least, I hoped he was faking it.

What came next was awful. It would take a lot to top a twerking Pat and Vanna in the awful department, but someone was clearly trying to break me.

Black-robed and hooded beings who appeared to have no feet floated into the room from behind the letterboard. There were three of them, and they each dragged a ghost on a glowing golden chain. I recognized the dead immediately and almost threw up in my mouth. It was Sam, John and Birdie. Their hollowed-out eyes were unfocused, and they seemed oblivious to the surroundings. It took everything I had and the help of my daughter and grandmother to keep me from charging the hooded bastards and destroying them.

"Not yet," Alana Catherine instructed. "This is a game. I have a feeling we can win them back."

I wasn't as sure. Normally, I looked before I leapt. Today I was running on raw emotion—that emotion being rage at the moment. However, my daughter was correct. I didn't know how someone who had little over a month of existence could be so wise, but she was a gift. My gift. Alone, this would have been a disaster. I wasn't alone. I was the present. Gram was the past and my child was the future. We were strongest together.

Nodding curtly, I took my place at the wheel. Sam, John and Birdie were led to a platform next to the letter board. Keeping my eye on them would be very easy.

"And the Angel of Mercy will spin first," Pat screamed, pointing at me.

"Rules?" I asked coldly. "Tell me the rules."

Vanna rolled her eyes and flipped me off. She was a nasty piece of work. "Spin the wheel and guess a damn letter. If you want to, you can try to solve the puzzle."

"Repercussions if I'm wrong?" I questioned in an even but steely tone.

"That one is a smart cookie!" Pat screeched as Vanna sneered at me. "If you guess wrong one of those deplorables turns to dust.

Again, Gram and Alana Catherine had to hold me back. It might not be the best move to fight physically, but no one said a war of the words was off the table.

"Interesting," I said. "I only see two deplorables in here."

Pat's eyes glazed over and Vanna yawned with boredom. Either they didn't realize I was referring to them or they didn't care. Didn't matter. It felt good to say it. Not as good as electrocuting the daylights out of them would have felt, but it would have to suffice.

"First word, three letters," Gram said, pointing to the board. "Second, three letters. Third, nine letters which is divisible by three. Last word, three letters. Three is our number, gals."

"No one guess the answer unless you're sure you know it," I instructed in a voice low enough Pat and Vanna couldn't hear me.

"What happens when we land on a name?" Alana Catherine questioned. "And what happens to the dead at the end of the game?"

They were excellent questions. "Pat Sajak," I called out as he and Vanna whisper-hissed viciously at each other. Maybe they weren't as tight as they appeared to be... "What happens to the dead at the end of the game?"

"If you solve the puzzle, and good luck with that, you get to keep them. If you *lose*... we get to keep them."

He was going to be lucky if he didn't *lose* his head in the very near future.

I needed to know one more detail. "And what happens when we land on an individual name?"

His expression turned sour. He was a colossal asshole.

"If you land on a name and the letter you pick is on the board, the owner of the name earns a point."

"And if the letter is not on the board?" I pressed.

He smiled. It was creepy. "They get a lash."

This was bullshit, but it didn't seem that there was a choice. Although...

"I'd like to take the lash in place of the dead," I stated flatly.

Vanna squealed with rabid delight. Pat trembled with excitement.

"YES!" he shouted.

Hustling over, he pulled me away from the wheel and over to the hooded bastards. They laughed as I was thrown to the ground at their feet. It was a slimy sound. This place was fucked.

Glancing over at Alana Catherine and Gram, I saw the fear on their faces. Unsure if I'd just given myself a death sentence, I reminded myself that if I died, I would come back. I gave them a thumbs-up and a forced smile.

"Let the games begin," Fake Pat Sajak bellowed.

My grandmother and daughter exchanged a few quiet words. When they parted, Gram was smiling like the cat who ate the canary. Alana Catherine gave me a covert thumbs up back, and I got a little worried. I didn't want either of them trading places with me. If that was their plan, I was going to kick their asses.

It wasn't their plan.

In a matter of five freaking minutes, I watched in delighted shock as every single time they guessed a letter it was correct. Every. Single. Time. All points, no lashes. It was uncanny luck or they were cheating. Pat and Vanna grew more perturbed with each correct guess and by the time there was only one letter left on the board, Pat was punching himself in the head, literally, and Vanna had clawed her arms until they bled.

It was every kind of awesome.

"I'd like to solve the fuckin' puzzle, Pat," Gram said, flipping the bruised and beaten man her middle finger.

Gram didn't flip birds. Gram did not use the F-bomb. That was then. This was now. She was badass.

"Go ahead, bitch," he shouted.

Gram smiled and waved at the skunks who were with her all the way. "May the strongest win."

"DAMNIT," Vanna shrieked. "Fine. They're yours, good fucking luck with the next round."

In a fit of fury, Fake Vanna White pulled a machine gun out from under one of the robes of the hooded freaks and opened fire on the skunks. They didn't stand a chance. I grabbed the ghosts and dove for Gram and Alana Catherine, tackling them to the ground and covering them with my body. The sounds of the skunks screaming in agony as Fake Pat, Fake Vanna and the woman with the headset made a run for it, make my stomach churn. The only solace I had was that the skunks would come back.

Slowly, I got off of Gram and Alana Catherine. The three of us along with Sam, Birdie and John stared at the remains of the massacre that had just taken place. It was so senseless and vile.

Alana Catherine shook like a leaf. The more my child trembled the more she began to glow. I'd expected her to glow either gold or red considering her parentage. That was not the case. The colors around my daughter were blinding and mix of every single color imaginable. Pandora had said she was much more than anyone knew. I was getting a preview to that right now.

I tried to reach out to comfort her, but the force of her power threw me back.

"This is wrong," she cried out. "So wrong. Come to me. I will care for you now."

"Oh shit," Gram muttered as the floor beneath us began to rock and buckle.

Shit was an understatement. All I could do was watch as my daughter tended to the slain adorable stinkers. As she chanted in the strange language Gideon had spoken earlier, I wondered if she understood the words. Regardless, the souls of the dead and torn-to-shreds mammals rose above the bloody murder site.

"Come to me," she commanded. "Come to me. NOW."

One by one, all fifty souls of the skunks flew into my daughter's body. She didn't flinch. She barely moved. Her arms were outstretched, and her magic swirled around her. I had no clue what the hell she was thinking. If she assumed that because Gram hopped a ride in me, that she could somehow bring the skunks to safety, we were going to have a serious talk.

"Well, slap my ass and call me Sally," Gram whispered in shock as Alana Catherine turned around and faced us with a huge smile on her face. "Our little gal is a Soul Keeper as well as the future Death Counselor."

"Wait. What?" I asked, sure I'd heard her wrong. That gift ran in bloodlines, just like the Death Counselor ran in ours. I was very sure that I'd given birth to her and that Gideon was her dad. Missy, who was a legit Soul Keeper, had nothing to do with it.

"That's not possible," I told Gram.

141

"Darlin," she said with a smile. "Anything is possible, you just have to believe."

My daughter approached us. "Don't be scared," she said. "It's all okay."

Sucking an audible breath in through my teeth, I shoved my hands into my pockets in frustration. "There might be a little problem."

She looked confused.

"Nothing dies here. It all comes back. What happens when all the souls you're housing come back to life?"

"Okay," Alana Catherine said in a higher pitch than I was used to hearing. "Wasn't aware of that wrinkle. You sure about that?"

"Positive," I replied.

"Fuck a duck," Gram muttered, using the F-bomb for the second time today. At the rate we were headed, she was going to make the Guinness Book of World Potty Mouth Records. Candy Vargo would be proud.

If I was my daughter, I'd be freaking out a little. I was not my daughter. She wasn't freaking out. She threw her head back and laughed.

"That's funny?" I asked warily.

She nodded. "Not to worry. When they want to regenerate, they're free to leave."

I wasn't positive, but I was pretty sure Gram dropped another F-bomb.

I walked over to my daughter and took her in my arms. "That was insane. Scared the heck out of me. I have a request."

"Shoot," she said, hugging me tight.

"Next time you're going to take a few centuries off my life, could I get a heads-up first, please?"

She giggled. "Yes. That's completely reasonable. Would you like to know what I'm going to do next?"

"Umm… I think so," I replied with a slight wince. "I mean, do I want to know?"

"You do," she assured me, walking over to Sam, John and Birdie. "I'm going to invite our dead friends into me to hang out with the skunks for a bit. They'll be safer that way."

To say I was stunned to silence would have been an understatement. My child was way ahead of all of us. Gideon was going to flip. I wasn't sure there was anything we could teach her that she didn't already know. Hell, she could probably teach us.

"That's a beautiful plan," I finally told her. "Sam, John and Birdie, please meet my daughter, Alana Catherine. She'd like to give you a safe haven until you can go back into the Light. Is that good?"

They were weak and fading. I wasn't sure if they'd understood what I'd just said. They had. With smiles of gratitude, they floated into Alana Catherine's open arms. The moment they made contact, they disappeared. It was simple and stunning.

"Can you feel 'em all in there?" Gram asked.

Alana Catherine smiled. "Kind of, but not physically. It's more of a spiritual knowledge that I'm their host."

Glancing around the stage, I noticed a door at the very back was lit up like a Christmas tree. It was beckoning to us.

"You gals ready for the second round?" I asked.

"Heck to the no," Gram said, patting both me and Alana Catherine on our heads. "But that ain't never stopped me and sure ain't gonna stop me today!"

Taking my daughter's hand in mine and Gram's in the other, we walked together toward the next round.

I spoke the message aloud for all or our benefits. "The game is a riddle. Three must play to win and break the evil spells. The show will go on and the wheels will turn. The answers are questions. The price must be right or the innocent will pay. In the end the choice will be on the strongest. The strongest shall emerge the victor. Anything is possible. You just have to believe. Time is running out."

"We've broken the evil spell," Alana Catherine said.

"And that there wheel did turn," Gram said, spitting on the wheel as we passed it.

"Then that means in the next game the answers will be questions," I said. "Anyone wanna take a guess what the game is?"

Gram gave me a salute. "What is *Jeopardy?*"

I had a feeling she was correct, and I would take the category of "Ready To Kick Ass" for five hundred, Alex.

CHAPTER TWELVE

THE *JEOPARDY* SOUNDSTAGE ON THE HIGHER POWER'S PLANE WAS identical to the one on human TV. As expected, there were three contestant podiums on the right side. The host stand was on the left, and the category board was in the middle on the back wall between the two. However, the board was dark, and no categories were listed. There was no audience in the studio like with *Wheel of Fortune*. Not trusting that, I kept my eyes peeled for a new set of armed mammals. I found nothing. The bleachers were empty.

"*Jeopardy!*" Gram exclaimed. "I love this show." She was positively giddy, considering the circumstances.

I wasn't giddy at all. The 'no category' and 'no audience' thing made me uneasy.

My gaze went to the setup on the empty stage.

"It's deserted in here," Alana Catherine pointed out with a small shudder.

"Not for long," I guessed. "You okay with all the guests inside you?"

She gave me a thumbs up. "Got room for a few more."

I knew what she was talking about. There were three more of the dead on my porch who hadn't been accounted for yet—Sister Catherine, Agnes and Steve. Something was gnawing at me. Why weren't there more? If there was a tear in the Light, wouldn't millions of souls be milling around in confusion? Wouldn't they have come looking for the Death Counselor? Wait. Not necessarily. Not all souls needed a Death Counselor. Most people didn't have unfinished business that kept them on the earthly plane after death. But... I'd helped send far more than six people into the Light. And over time, Gram had sent hundreds into the Light. Why hadn't they all come back?

And where in the hell was the Higher Power? Cecily said she'd seen It immediately. Granted, she hadn't known it was the Higher Power at first. Had that happened to me as well? I'd be hard-pressed to believe Fake Pat Sajak or Fake Vanna White were the Higher Power. That left the harried assistant whose name I didn't know. Alana Catherine had been firm in her belief that the woman wasn't the Higher Power, but if she wasn't, then who was?

As I wrestled with my thoughts, Gram took my hand in hers and gave it a quick squeeze. "Come on back from where you went, darlin'," she said. "We need to stay focused on the now. I'm expectin' Fake Alex Trebek to show up any minute now doin' the hula in his birthday suit."

I squeezed back and smiled. "You're right—although, I really hope he's not naked." I looked around again. We were still the only people here. "What should we do while we wait for whatever crazy is headed our way?"

"Welp, I say we keep our minds as sharp as tacks!" Gram said, pushing me over to the podiums. "A little practice never hurt nobody. Alana Catherine, get your cutie patootie over here. We're gonna bone up."

"Yikes," Alana Catherine said as Gram led her to a podium.

"Now, y'all can call me Alexa Trebek!" Gram said with a giggle as she stepped behind the host console. "I'm gonna give out an answer, and you're gonna give me the question. Got it?"

"Got it," I told her.

"Alrighty then," Gram said, clearing her throat. She took her game shows seriously. When she started humming the theme song to *Jeopardy,* I had to groan. The old lady was tone-deaf. When she finished, she took a bow in front of the imaginary audience and then shouted at the top of her lungs—"This is *Jeopardy!*"

Apparently, we were ready to start.

"The answer is… Whale of Fortune," Gram announced with a mischievous little grin.

"Did you say whale?" I asked, unsure if I'd misheard.

"Daisy," she admonished me. "That right there would get you disqualified. If you ask a question, it's gotta be the question to the answer."

I scrunched up my nose and glanced over at my daughter, who seemed as perplexed as I was.

"I'm pretty sure she said whale," Alana Catherine told me.

"Ain't no conspirin' with the other contestant," Gram yelled. "Lordy have mercy, ain't y'all ever watched *Jeopardy?*"

"Actually, no," Alana Catherine said with a laugh. "I'm pretty sure I've never watched any TV at all yet."

"That's true," I said. "You're only a little over a month old. You're more interested in my boob and your thumb than TV. And it's been a while since I've watched *Jeopardy.*"

Gram slapped herself in the forehead. "My bad, sweeties. I

feel like we've been busier than a cat coverin' up poop on a cement floor. I'm gettin' ahead of myself. Lemme take both parts of the first clue to help you understand how the game is played."

"Excellent thinking, Gram," Alana Catherine said.

"Okay, so if the answer is Whale of Fortune, then the question you should ask is, 'What game show do fish watch?' Get it?"

"Sadly, yes," I said with a giggle. "Try another."

"And the answer is, Cat-has-trophy."

Alana hit the buzzer first. "What do you call it when a cat wins *Jeopardy*?"

"YES!" Gram squealed.

I glanced over at my daughter in awe. "Is there anything you can't do?"

She nodded. "Tie my shoes. You haven't taught me that yet."

"Yes! There *is* something I can teach you," I said, pumping my fists over my head.

My beautiful child laughed. "Yes, there is, Mom. However, I wouldn't be pumping my fists over my head if I were you... So far, I'm winning this round of *Jeopardy*."

I raised a brow. She copied my look. There was no way in this Universe I could love her more than I did right now. "Fine. Challenge accepted. Gram, throw out another answer."

"Will do! The answer is, Let's Make a Dill!"

Alana slapped her buzzer. "What is a pickle's favorite game show?"

"Heck to the yeseroonie!" Gram squealed.

"How did you come up with that?" I asked, wildly confused. "You've never seen Let's Make a Deal."

"Logical deduction," Alana Catherine replied. "Gram loves

game shows, so I figured all the questions would be game show-specific. She loves pickles, referenced by her use of the phrase, that just dills my pickle. She also told a pickle joke to the skunks. I figured with the word dill in the answer and Gram's love of pickles that I was on the right track."

"Freaking genius! My daughter is a freaking genius."

Alana Catherine rolled her eyes, but her smile was wide. She was getting a pet skunk even if Gideon didn't want one. He wasn't the only one she had wrapped around her finger.

"Darn tootin'," Gram agreed. "You sugar pies wanna do a couple more to get into the rhythm?"

"I think we'd better since Mom is losing so badly," Alana Catherine stated, then pursed her lips playfully.

"Get ready to go down, little girl," I challenged, waggling my brows.

"I'd like to see you try," she shot right back with a grin.

"And the answer is, Wheel of Fortune Cookies," Gram announced.

"I know," I shouted as Alana Catherine slapped her buzzer.

"Whoopsiedoodle," Gram said, wagging her finger at me. "You gotta use the buzzer, little missy. Alana Catherine, what's the question?"

"What do you call a game show in a Chinese restaurant?"

"WOOHOO!" Gram yelled as she did a little boogie around her console. "That's the correct question. Three to nothin'. Our baby girl is winnin'!"

I didn't care if my baby girl beat me at games for the rest of her life. It would make me proud. However, Gram was smart to have us practice. I wasn't good at this at all. "One more," I begged. "Give me the chance to redeem myself just a tiny bit."

"Not a problem," Gram said, scratching her head to come

up with another. "Try this one on for size! The answer is, The Newly Web Game."

I slammed down on the buzzer and came in barely before my child. She winked and graciously gave me the floor.

"What's a spider's favorite game show?" I crowed, taking a bow before Gram could confirm my answer.

Alana Catherine clapped and Gram ran over to give me a high five. "Correct," she yelled.

Our celebration was cut short by the harried woman with the headset from earlier. "For the love of losers," she muttered, looking us up and down with disgust and dismay. "You three again? You couldn't have changed your clothes?"

Her attitude was starting to chap my ass. While it would have been satisfying in the moment to have a vicious go at her outfit, I went right back to my Southern roots. Winning the long game was better than getting gratification in the short one. "Well, bless your heart. It must seem like we don't know whether to check our asses or scratch our watches, but you know all about that since that's obviously the way you live."

She was confused. It was glorious. I kept going.

"And I don't care what anybody says, it's fine to think you're pretty in your own way. And if anyone tells you that your biscuit isn't done in the middle, just ignore it. They might be right, but rude is rude. You get me?"

"Umm…" The gal was at a loss for words.

I was not. Gram was loving it. She'd taught me well. "You know, you might be a little rough around the edges, but I heard there was one person who said you have got just the best personality."

"What?" she asked, trying to figure out if I was complimenting her or insulting her.

"You just keep marching to your own drummer," I told her,

giving her two thumbs up and the most insincere smile I had in me. "Good for you! Good for you!"

I'd flustered her. She opened her mouth twice to come back at me. Twice, she closed it. As she turned to leave, she called out over her shoulder. "Five minutes until the show begins."

The board lit up, and my head began to throb. There were only three rows. One row was labeled Sister Catherine. The next was labeled Agnes Bubbala, and the third was labeled Riddles.

The face of Sister Catherine popped up in my mind. My daughter's middle name was in honor of the lovely woman. Before I really knew Sister Catherine, I'd nicknamed her the Tasmanian Devil. She was batshit nuts as a ghost and totally out of control. She'd been forty-seven when she'd died of cancer. It broke my heart how young she was when she'd died. She had no regrets. Said she'd lived a very full and happy life. She'd been a nun. At first, it had been hard to reconcile that the gal who liked to moon people and pop out of my silverware drawer when I least expected had been a woman of faith.

Through talking with each other and eventually diving into her mind, I determined that Sister Catherine had no unfinished business. None. Nothing. She was the one who realized she was here to help me. She was unselfish and all about others in life. She was the same way in death. It was with tremendous joy and gratitude that I named my child after her.

Sister Catherine's final wish before she'd gone into the Light was to be mooned by all of us. It was the most bizarre and hilarious request I'd gotten from one of the dead. I was all in. Of course, Candy Vargo had been delighted to show her ass. Even Gideon very reluctantly agreed because of his friendship with the nutty nun. It was a moment in time that would be etched in my mind and heart no matter how long I lived.

Alana Catherine was named for my mom, Alana, and the infamous Tasmanian Devil who I adored. It was a good strong name for a beautiful and strong young woman… who used to be a baby less than a few hours ago. Part of me was desperate for her to still be a baby when we got back home. But part of me would miss the young woman I loved just as much as her baby version.

Glancing over at my daughter, I tried to memorize her face so that if she reverted back to a baby when we got home, I'd remember. She was staring at the board. I joined her.

Agnes Bubbla's name was the next row over. The dead woman was someone I considered a friend. Agnes was a New York Times best-selling paranormal romance author. She was also Candy Vargo's favorite writer. Candy had flipped her shit when she'd realized Agnes was with us. She'd driven Agnes nuts, but the woman was a good sport about it. She was kind-hearted and funny as heck. Her personal style had gotten stuck in the 1980's—dyed blonde hair with bangs that defied gravity. Her terms of endearment still made me smile—puddin', cupcake, sweet pea and pumpkin were my faves.

My dear Agnes had been murdered by the psychotic son of a bitch, Micky Muggles. She'd died of a heart attack caused by a potassium overdose. That bastard was gone now. He wasn't in the Darkness and he wasn't in the Light. He wasn't even good enough for Purgatory. He was just gone, never to be heard from again. Hatred was a strong word and took energy. Normally, I did my best not to feel hate in my heart. But Micky Muggles was the exception. Him… I hated.

Agnes belonged in the Light. She might be dead but her books would make her as Immortal as a human could get.

Squaring my shoulders, I left memory lane behind and planted myself firmly in the present. I was going to win back

Sister Catherine and Agnes. And after I'd fixed the tear in the Light, I would send them back home. Period.

A booming male voice came over the speaker, and the lights hanging over the stage brightened.

"This is *Jeopardy*! Entering the studio… Well, crap. They're already on the stage. Who's running this shitty show?"

I glanced around to see who was talking, but no one but Gram, Alana Catherine and me were here.

"Anyway," the male voice snapped. "Today's rude contestants are the three women standing on the stage. Where in the hell are my notes?" he bellowed. "I'm supposed to have notes with the names of the damn contestants on them. Somebody is getting FIRED."

He stopped talking for a second. My guess was that the voice was either composing itself or went to go find his notes and fire the staff.

"I'm back," the voice shouted. "And now… entering the fucking studio like he's supposed to do, is the host of *Jeopardy*! Alex Trebek."

And what to my wondering eyes should appear? A mostly naked Alex Trebek wearing a hula skirt. I gave Gram the side eye.

"This is your fault, old lady," I told her, trying to bite back my laugh of horror.

"I know that," she said, shaking her head. "But you did conjure up them skunks."

"True," I confirmed. "But they were a hell of a lot cuter than Alex in a grass skirt."

"Fine," Gram said with a giggle. "You win, Daisy girl. But Alex does have a nice smattering of gray chest hair, if I do say so myself."

I raised a brow. "You're courting Mr. Jackson," I reminded her.

"A girl can still look," she told me with a grin.

"Welcome to *Jeopardy*, assholes," Alex Trebek said in a voice that was not Alex Trebek's.

We were back to the fakes. I just hope this Fake Alex Trebek wasn't as randy as Fake Pat Sajak. I didn't think my digestive system could handle it.

"Here's the deal," Fake Alex said sounding like he was about to take a nap. "I give the answer. You ask the question. You stupid idiots have to get all of them correct or you don't win your ghosts back. Capiche?"

"Yes," I said. "Do we get to pick the category?"

He gave me a scathing glare. It made me want to electrocute the jackass. I refrained. It was difficult but doable. I wanted to set a good example for my daughter. Just because someone was a douche didn't mean that one should immediately resort to violence. Of course, if Fake Alex threw the first punch, I'd take him out without breaking a sweat.

"Are you braindead?" he demanded, pointing at the board.

There was only one row lit up now. The Agnes and Sister Catherine rows were gone. I wasn't sure what that meant, but it didn't feel right.

"When I got here, there were three categories. Where did they go?" I questioned the nasty man.

"I guess they fell apart," he replied with an evil laugh. "You got a problem with that?"

"Potentially," I replied. "However, I guess we'll just wait and see."

He yawned. "I guess we will."

Gram was very disappointed in one of her favorite hosts. She wore the expression of a woman who'd just swallowed a lemon. Alana Catherine was calm and composed. I was teetering close to losing my shit, but at least I wasn't wearing a hula skirt.

"Get to it!" the announcer's voice boomed through the speakers.

"I am," Fake Alex yelled. "First answer, what comes but never arrives?"

Gram hit her buzzer first. "What is tomorrow, Alex?"

"Correct, imbecile," he said. "Next, what can be broken but never held?"

Alana Catherine was quickest on the draw. "What is a promise, Alex?"

He rolled his eyes. "That's the right answer, halfwit."

Fake Alex Trebek was a dick. My podium was in the middle, between my gals. Pulling them close, I gave them the new modus operandi. "If he's a dick, we're going to dick him right back. Got it?"

Alana Catherine grinned and nodded. Gram gave me a thumbs up and a giggle. It was time to dick the dick.

"Next," Alex said with his eyes closed.

Was he about to fall asleep? This was crazy.

He scowled. "What goes up, but never comes down?"

I Buffalo Billed my buzzer and came out on top. "What is age, shit stain?"

Old Alex woke right up after that one. His eyes narrowed and he looked like he might throw a tantrum. The jerk could dish it out but clearly couldn't take it.

"That is correct, simpleton."

"Thanks, douche canoe," I replied.

His eyes opened wide and the announcer laughed through his mic.

"Moron," he snapped.

"Cocksucker," Alana Catherine chimed in, much to Fake Alex's horror.

I winced at the word 'cocksucker'. Where in the heck did she learn that? It had to have been Candy Vargo. I was going to help Gram wash Candy's mouth out with soap in the very near future.

"Ignoramus," Alex growled.

"You can kiss my go to hell," Gram ground out. "You peckerhead."

Fuck this," Fake Alex said, throwing his notes into the air. "I don't get paid enough to deal with this shit. You cretins win. You can have your fucking ghosts. What do I care?"

The man-baby stomped off the stage, but right before he was out of sight, he turned back and smiled. It was oily and vicious. "Your ghosts are behind the board. You'll have exactly five minutes to put the pieces together and remove them from the studio or they'll turn to dust. Good luck, wankers."

And on that note, Fake Alex left the building.

"What was all that gibberish about?" Gram asked. "I tell you what, that man was so nasty I wouldn't walk across the street to piss on him if he was on fire."

"That's very colorful," Daisy said, putting her arm around Gram.

"Thanks, darlin'. I'm good that way."

I moved quickly to the area behind the board. What I saw made me furious and want to sob at the same time. There were two piles on the ground—piles of body parts. One belonged to Sister Catherine and the other to Agnes Bubbala.

"No. No, no, no, no, no," I said, dropping to my knees and snapping my fingers to conjure up some superglue. "I can do this. I have to do this."

My stomach dropped further when I realized the piles

might not be correct. It was difficult to tell what belonged to Agnes and which parts were Sister Catherine's. Whoever planned this was psychotic.

Less than four minutes were left. Staring at the piles wasn't going to work. "I'm just going to start gluing and hope for the best." My voice was thick with unshed tears. Why in the world would anyone be this shitty?

As I desperately searched for a hand that would match the arm I held, I felt my daughter's gentle touch on my back.

"Mom, stop," she said.

"Can't," I told her as I crawled into the middle of the piles and searched harder. "I can't let them turn to dust. It's not fair."

"Mom," Alana Catherine said in a sterner tone. "Stop. Now." I turned my head to look at her. Her voice may have been harsh, but her eyes were gentle. "Do you trust me?"

Immediately, I nodded. "With my life."

"Then you have to stop and back away. I've got this," she said.

Stepping back wasn't in my nature, especially when something so dire was on the line—like the afterlives of two of my friends. However, I did. I stepped back and held my breath.

Without a second to lose, my daughter—the future Death Counselor and apparently the future Soul Keeper—went to work. Alana Catherine got down on her knees and gathered all the parts together with care. She then waved her arms above the broken bodies of the two women.

It wasn't fancy. It didn't include any bells or whistles, but... it worked.

In less time than it took me to blink, Agnes and Sister Catherine were whole. I wanted to scream with joy and talk to them for hours, but that wasn't on the agenda. There was one minute left in the five that Fake Alex Trebek had given us. If we didn't get the gals out of the studio, they'd turn to dust.

"We have to go," I insisted. "Agnes, Sister Catherine, this is my daughter, Alana Catherine."

"It's nice to meet you ladies," Alana Catherine said.

"Same here, puddin'," Agnes said as clear as day with a big smile on her face.

She was a ghost, but didn't sound like one.

"Oh my," Sister Catherine said as she wrapped her transparent arms around me. "Thank you very much, my friend. I owe you one."

"You owe me nothing," I told her as I corralled the two ladies towards my daughter's open arms. "Not only is my child the future Death Counselor, she's also the future Soul Keeper."

"Yep," Alana Catherine said with a warm smile. "And I'd be honored to host you for a bit until we can safely take you back into the Light."

"Sounds like a plan, pumpkin," Agnes said, floating straight into my child's arms.

"I'm good with that," Sister Catherine agreed.

"Hurry up, friends," I insisted. "We've got less than a minute to get out of here."

The ladies listened. They were safely inside my daughter.

"Have to get out of here," I said, grabbing my grandma and daughter's hands.

"Where to?" Gram asked as we stood in the middle of the stage.

Glancing around wildly for the right way to go, my eyes landed on a door. It was lit up like the Fourth of July. The answer was obvious. What was behind the door wasn't. I knew how to find out.

"Everybody ready for round three?" I asked, running to the exit with my girls by my side.

"Hell to the yes," Gram yelled. "Bring it on!"

"What she said," Alana Catherine added.

Three was our magic number. I knew in my gut three things—One, this would be the final test. Two, I'd find Steve behind that door, and three, it was time to end the Higher Power's games. I just hoped the coward would show up because I had a hell of a lot to say.

CHAPTER THIRTEEN

To no one's great surprise, we walked onto the set of *The Price is Right*. Gram squealed with delight. *The Price is Right* was her crack and she'd always jokingly referred to Bob Barker as her boyfriend when she was alive. Her obsession was real. In death, the Game Show Channel was on 24/7 at my house, and she watched the reruns of the show religiously. She'd seen all the episodes so many times she could tell you the winner of the Final Showcase by who would be picked as contestants at the top of the episode. It was sweet, nutty and vintage Gram.

After she'd run around the set, touching all the props with childlike excitement, she stopped abruptly. Her chin dropped to her chest, and I thought she was going to cry.

Alana Catherine and I rushed over.

"Gram, talk to me," I said, wrapping my arms around her. "Tell me what's wrong."

"Aww, Daisy girl," she said, swiping at a tear rolling down her cheek. "I'm sorry. Seein' my Nirvana in person for the first time is kinda overwhelmin'. My heart's just breakin' up knowin' that my old boyfriend, Bob Barker, is probably gonna be a giant jackhole in this version."

"It's okay, Gram," Alana Catherine said, joining the hug. "Whoever shows up today isn't going to be the real Bob Barker."

Gram rested her chin on my shoulder and sighed. "I know. And I know I'm actin' all the fool. We got way bigger problems than the disappointment of an old lady who's addicted to game shows."

"You're not a problem," I said firmly. "Everything is relative and feelings are real. It's fine to have them. Get them out now, so we'll be ready."

She kissed my cheek and nodded. "Just gimme a few minutes to get over myself," she said with a small, embarrassed giggle. "I'll be right and ready in a hot sec."

I nodded to my daughter, and we both gave Gram a little space to mourn the loss of what was about to happen. Taking my child's hand in mine, we walked away to inspect the area.

Again, we were the only live people on the soundstage. However, the bleachers were filled with cardboard cutouts of audience members.

"Umm... is this weird or am I crazy?" Alana Catherine inquired as we stared at the hundred or so women and men with crazed expressions of anticipation and fevered eagerness on their paper faces.

"We're both crazy, but this is extremely weird," I acknowledged.

We stood in silence for a long moment and checked out the creepy crowd.

Turning away, I shuddered. "That's giving me the heebie-jeebies."

"Word," my daughter agreed.

Gram was doing jumping jacks to shake it off. The visual made me smile. When we got home—and we were going to get home—she'd be a ghost again. I realized that I hadn't taken any time to appreciate the good amidst all the scary and bad. I was pretty sure my twenty-year-old daughter would be a baby again and I was missing out on really getting to know this version of her no matter how brief it might be. Granted, we were sort of busy trying to save lives and make sure we didn't lose our own, but once a moment disappeared it was gone for good.

"I need to live in the now," I said aloud.

"What?" Alana Catherine asked, confused.

Turning to face her, I cupped her face in my hands. "I want you to know this. I love you. I love you more than I thought it was possible to love anyone. You're such a gift to me and your dad. He's completely besotted with you."

She squinted at me. "Are we getting ready to die or something?"

"I seriously hope not," I told her with a chuckle. "But if we do, we'll come back. Nothing stays dead on the Higher Power's plane." I paused and tried to find the right words to explain myself. "Our lives are long. Immortals live forever, but forever is too long to grasp. It's the small exchanges and split seconds of joy that make a life—not the length of it. If we stop acknowledging those moments, then life isn't worth living. I have no idea what's about to go down. But my gut tells me that this is the last game. I just need you to know how much you mean to me."

My little girl, who wasn't so little, threw herself at me and hugged me hard. The feeling was glorious. I sniffed her head like I did earlier today when she was a baby, and she smelled just as delicious.

"You are so very special, Alana Catherine," I whispered against her head. "So very loved."

"So are you," she replied. "And I love you more."

I laughed. "Not possible."

"Is," she countered.

"Not," I shot back. "I'd die for you."

She pulled back and looked me in the eye. "And I'd die for you."

She was serious. That didn't sit well. The order was all wrong. "Not happening. Ever."

She grinned and booped my nose. "That goes both ways, Mom. Let's just try and stay alive. Deal?"

My girl was something else. She was truly far more than any of us knew. "Deal."

"Alrightyroo," Gram said, joining us. "How about a little tutorial of the games on the show?"

"Genius," I said. I was sure that Steve was the prize. There was no losing this round. That was unacceptable.

Gram grabbed our hands and hustled us onto the stage. "You ready?"

"Born that way," Alana Catherine said with a lopsided grin. "Let's get this party started."

I was still amazed at how much my daughter knew and understood. It was like she'd been some kind of omnipresent figure in all of our lives. The feeling was unsettling and worried me, but that conversation would have to wait. Just having her with me was enough. Whoever she was meant to be would emerge eventually. Gideon and I would be by her side every step of the way.

Gram pointed to a large pegged board. It was slanted and had a bunch of pegs arranged in uneven rows. "That right there is called Plinko. You're gonna get you some chips and drop 'em down the board from the top. If you drop it down the middle, you're more likely to win the big cash prizes."

"The prizes aren't cash," Alana Catherine pointed out quietly.

She was right, and when I glanced down at the bottom of the board, my stomach roiled. The prize was a person. A person who was near and dear to my heart—a part of me. The man who had been my husband and who'd been murdered by Clarissa. The heinous former Angel of Mercy had done her best to make it look like an accident... a suicide. The truth had eventually come out, but it was too late for Steve.

I'd loved him, and he'd loved me. I still loved him, but not like I loved Gideon. Gideon was my soulmate. The man I was going to spend eternity with. Steve had been my first love, but it wasn't a real marriage, so to speak. While he'd loved me as a best friend, he wasn't capable of loving me as a romantic partner. I'd spent many years wondering what was wrong with me. It had messed with my self-esteem and self-worth. But it hadn't been me. My husband, who'd grown up in an abusively religious household, had been gay. Something he wasn't able to admit to himself or to me in life. However, in death, he came back. I was his unfinished business, and he was devastated that he'd lied to both of us for so long. His mission before he could leave the earthly plane was to help me find the love that I deserved. The love he wasn't able to give to me.

It had devastated and infuriated me initially. But my love for Steve transcended any long-term anger. In the end, I was as heartbroken as he was that he hadn't been able to live his true, authentic life. His friendship and love for all those years shaped me into the woman I was today. He would hold a top place in my and Gideon's hearts forever.

Sending my best friend back into the Light was imperative. It was where he belonged.

"I don't like them odds," Gram huffed, looking at the board. Steve's name was there three times. The other three slots were empty of a name. "What happens if the chip don't land on Steve?'

I had no answer. I didn't want to consider it. I pointed to another game. "What's that one?"

Gram and Alana Catherine exchanged concerned glances but didn't say anything. We walked across the stage to the next game.

"That one is called Cliffhangers," Gram explained. "That there little mountain climber guy is the key to winnin' or losin'. Bob, or Fake Bob, is gonna show you an item. If you get the price right that little climber man stays where he is. If you get it wrong, he starts climbing up the mountain. If he gets to the top and falls off the cliff, you lose."

"Seems kind of violent," Alana Catherine commented.

I didn't disagree. Leaning in, I took a closer look at the little mountain climber guy and gasped. He was a small replica of Steve.

"Oh my God," I said.

"What's wrong?" Gram asked.

I pointed at the little man. "It's Steve. The mountain man looks like Steve.

Gram closed her eyes and pressed the bridge of her nose. "Lemme apologize up front."

"For?" Alana Catherine asked.

"For this," Gram replied. She stomped her feet and punched the board. "This is FUCKED," she shouted, then took a dramatic pause. "That. That was what I was apologizin' for."

"No need," I told her. It occurred to me that Steve would

have laughed his head off to hear Gram cuss. He had the most wonderful sense of humor and adored Gram.

Our odds of winning Steve back were growing slimmer with each game. The Higher Power was screwing with me. What I needed to know was why. What was the benefit of sending me over the edge? It was supposed to be some kind of benevolent being. So far, It seemed like a huge gaping narcissistic asshole. I didn't understand the game. And I still couldn't wrap my head around why only six dead had come back from the Light. If there was a tear in the Light, there should be millions, if not trillions, roaming around.

"Why haven't we seen the Higher Power yet?" I asked. Since I didn't know the answer, maybe one of the others did.

"Maybe we have," Gram said. "Kill me now if it was that horny Fake Pat Sajak."

"Or the perpetually pissed-off Fake Alex Trebek," Alana Catherine added with a shake of her head.

"If it was Fake Vanna White, I'm quitting. It doesn't seem worth it if the Higher Power wears spanks and twerks," I commented.

Gram cackled. Alana Catherine looked shocked for a beat before she threw her head back and laughed. I joined them. It was insanely inappropriate to laugh considering the circumstances, but the release was cathartic.

"Alana Catherine, are you sure the stage manager gal wasn't the Higher Power?" I asked.

Her brow wrinkled in thought. "I was sure of it when I said it, but now... I don't know."

"Does it matter?" Gram asked.

It was a good question that I didn't have an answer to. The Higher Power would reveal Itself when It wanted to be seen. It was as cryptic as the rest of the Immortals. Being older than time made many of those who lived forever lose it. Some truly lost their minds and went off the deep end like Zadkiel had. Others lost touch with reality and humanity. It was tragic and very dangerous. I didn't know where the Higher Power sat in that spectrum, but with someone who was thought of as the supreme leader of all, it could certainly go to Its head... or worse.

"Next game, please," I said, pushing all the dark thoughts away and putting my focus where it needed to be.

Gram obliged. She walked us over to a huge wheel. I'd seen this one when I'd watched the show with her over the years.

"This one right here is called the Big Wheel Game," she said, pointing at it. "On the show you spin that wheel and try to get as close to one dollar as you can without goin' over. You get two spins."

"Problem," Alana Catherine said, pointing at the wheel. "All of the amounts are already over a dollar."

Gram lost it. Candy Vargo would have been left speechless by the profane tirade the old woman went on. I was left with my mouth hanging open. Alana Catherine was stunned to shocked silence. It lasted well over a minute, and I heard some combinations of words I wasn't aware could exist together. Actually, they should never exist together, but it was quite the crude and filthy education.

When Gram was finished, she grinned like she'd won first prize. "Welp, sorry about that, but I now get why my Candy Vargo likes to express herself with poop words. Sometimes them are the only words that accurately depict real feelings. You know what I mean?"

"Umm... yes. That was very colorful, Gram," I said.

"Sure was," she said, blowing out a long breath. "Took a few years off my life, but since I'm already dead, I figure that don't matter."

"Right," I said, letting her tirade sink in and trying not to burst into laughter.

"But," she said, getting serious. "I think this is a setup. Ain't no way we can win Steve back with those rigged games."

Alana Catherine stepped into the conversation. "I think that's part of the master plan. The Higher Power wants something else."

"Like what?" I asked, agreeing with her and hoping against hope she knew what the gaping ass wanted.

"That's the game," she said with a frustrated sigh. "At least, I think it is. Maybe It wants you, Mom."

That was an alarming thought. Was the problem that I held more than one job? I was both the Angel of Mercy and the Death Counselor. Was my power a threat? Was It that insane? Originally, I didn't want any of the jobs that had been forced on me. Now? Now was a different story. I was honored to have both of them. If It had a problem with that, It could shove it up Its ass… if It had an ass. Cecily had seen the Higher Power as a person named Phyllis. I'd seen nothing here that even remotely resembled Phyllis. But that was expected. Everyone saw their own version of the Higher Power… except me. It might not be a person at all.

Gram paced the stage and let a few extra profanities drop here and there. When we got home, everyone was in for a foul surprise.

"All this has got me to thinkin," Gram said. She stopped her pacing and faced us. "I don't think there's no hole in the Light."

I felt a little dizzy with relief. She'd just verbalized what had been running through my mind. "Why?" I asked. "Tell me why you think that."

She walked over and pulled the three of us into a huddle. "Any of y'all find it weird that only six ghosts have come back if there's a rip in the Light?"

"I did think that was odd," Alana Catherine admitted.

"So did I," I said. "So, if there's no tear in the Light, that would mean the Higher Power stole innocent souls from the Light. I don't understand the endgame."

"Unless my guess was right," Alana Catherine said. "Maybe getting you to come here to Its plane was the game all along."

"Why?" I pressed. "Why would having me here be the endgame?'

No one knew the answer.

"Five minutes until the show starts," the harried stage manager yelled, startling all three of us. "Get ready to lose, losers."

She grinned and walked back into the wings.

"Southern ladies don't lose," Gram ground out. "We get even. You hear me, girls?"

"Loud and clear," I said.

Alana Catherine took the lead. "If they cheat, we cheat. If they go low, we go lower. Goal is Steve's soul. If we have to play dirty, we'll play dirty. If the Higher Power wants to spar, we leave the bastard headless. We're not messing around, and nothing dies here permanently."

I jumped on the bandwagon. "Gram, if the going gets tuff, I want you to let loose with some of those cuss words. That was the most disgusting crap I've ever heard, and it would make a brilliant distraction."

My daughter nodded. "Also, just a heads up, the skunks are getting restless. In exchange for me giving them safe harbor, they're willing to asphyxiate the Higher Power if we need to make a quick getaway."

I was thrown a little sideways by the violence of my daughter's plan. It was the weirdest battle plan I'd heard to date, but to be fair, this was the weirdest situation I'd ever been in. There was a reason all three of us were here. Maybe this was it.

"We're in this together." I took Gram and Alana Catherine's hands and gave them a squeeze. "You with me?

"Until the end," my child replied.

"The bitter end," Gram added with determination.

My lips tugged up as I bared my teeth in what felt like a feral grin. "Turn up the music and light the fireworks," I growled. "This party is about to pop off."

"Like the Higher Power's head," Alana Catherine added on a snarl.

My eyes widened. My daughter had her father's penchant for violence and my dogged determination to do whatever it took to get the job done.

"What?" Alana Catherine shrugged and gave me a sheepish smile. "Nothing's impossible, including decapitating the Higher Power, if you believe."

I chuckled. "I believe," I told her. "I believe."

The Higher Power was the creator of all things, and I wasn't foolish enough to believe that defeating It would be a cakewalk, but Alana Catherine's faith in me—in us—gave me hope.

And for now, that would have to be enough.

CHAPTER FOURTEEN

GRAM POINTED TO THE BLEACHERS. "THERE ARE THREE OPEN seats in the front row. Come on."

We followed her over and sat amongst the cardboard audience.

"Why don't we just stay on the stage?" I asked. "We know we're going to be chosen as the contestants."

"Not how the game works," she said. "We're gonna play by the rules until the Higher Power breaks 'em."

I didn't question her wisdom. We were a triad—the past, the present, and the future. In order to come out on top, the power of three was the law.

The theme song blasted through the speakers. It was loud, and I slapped my hands over my ears. Normally, the tune made me smile. It reminded me of Gram. Today, it was terrifying.

The same announcer voice from *Jeopardy* bellowed through the sound system. "This is *The Price is Right!* Gram, come on down!"

Gram stood, pumped her skinny arms over her head, and

ran down to one of the three podiums on the floor at the edge of the stage.

The announcer wasn't done. "Alana Catherine, come on down!"

My daughter mimicked her great-grandmother with the fist pump and ran to the second podium.

And the final call came. "Daisy, come on down!"

It was painful to act excited, but I did it. However, I did it my way. Instead of fists over my head, I shot the bird with both hands in the air while I ran down to my podium. The little acts of defiance were getting me through this trial and keeping me from becoming unhinged.

With flashing lights and canned cheers, Bob Barker walked out onto the stage. I'd expected him to have attractive girls with him who displayed the items during the show, but he was alone. It was suspect, but I kept my cool. Jumping to conclusions wouldn't help the cause.

Bob Barker bared his teeth at us in what I think he thought was a smile. It wasn't.

"That's a Fake Bob," Gram said under her breath. "My Bob had a lovely smile. This guy looks like he just swallowed a turd whole."

I almost choked on my spit. Gram had a way with words like no one else. She was also correct. Fake Bob Barker wasn't happy to see us. He snapped his fingers, and a human-sized box wrapped in shiny silver paper lowered from the ceiling. It was released to the floor with a thud. Bob walked over to the box and stared at it for about a minute too long. None of the other hosts had used magic. Fake Bob was no ordinary host.

I knew what was in that box—or rather, who was in that box. It was Steve. I could feel his energy. The desire to just take the box, Gram and Alana Catherine and leave this fucked up plane was intense. My daughter, recognizing my inclination, placed her hand in mine and squeezed.

"Not yet," she whispered. "Soon, but not yet."

I nodded jerkily. I pushed back my emotional rage and concentrated on the logistical aspects. Emotions made one sloppy in battle. There was no room for error, and I wasn't going to be the catalyst for failure.

Fake Bob slowly turned to the audience and made direct eye contact with me. His eyes flashed silver and gold. It was usually stunning and something I'd never seen. I was positive we were finally in the Higher Power's presence. It was time to start playing the real game. Not knowing what it was or the rules were was dangerous, but we were here to win.

"You will play the games," he demanded with a sly little smirk playing on his lips. "You must win all of them to walk away with the silver box."

"And if we don't?" I question flatly.

If he didn't like my tone, he didn't show it. "Then I win the box and what's inside."

"I call bullshit," I said, as canned gasps came through the speakers. I rolled my eyes and stood my ground. "The games are rigged."

Fake Bob feigned surprise. No one was buying what he was selling. "Now why would you say that, Daisy?" he questioned, pouting. "You seem to be holding a grudge against me. So unnecessary and not to your benefit."

I shrugged and smiled. My smile threw him off a bit. "Some people might call it holding a grudge. I call it, I see who you are and am choosing not to unsee it. I'm free to choose, Bob."

His brows shot up and his eyes flashed dangerously. "Freedom of choice does not mean freedom of consequences."

"Exactly," I said with an exaggerated wink. "I do believe you might want to keep that in mind."

The stare-down was extreme. Neither one of us wanted to be the first to break it. His utter surprise that I didn't back down made the disgusting man or whatever he was chuckle.

"Your reputation precedes you quite accurately," he finally said.

"As does yours," I shot back.

"And what might my reputation be?" he inquired casually. There was nothing casual about the question.

"I'm not one to gossip," I replied evenly. "I could turn the question back on you."

"That would be rude."

"I have to respectfully refute that statement. I have excellent manners. Would you like to know how I know that?" I asked.

He was curious. Clearly perturbed, but curious. "But of course."

"The definition of good manners in my book is putting up with the bad manners of others."

He didn't like my answer. I didn't like him. We were even.

His eyes narrowed to slits. "Play the game or I will destroy the box."

"Show me what's in the box," I challenged.

He smiled. It came nowhere close to reaching his eyes. The Higher Power made my blood run cold. This wasn't a benevolent being. *It* was a crime against humanity. How had we gotten to this?

With great fanfare and more loud music from the speakers, Fake Bob removed the paper from the box and then clapped his hands. The box disintegrated, and Steve stood in his ghostly form on the stage. He wasn't out of it. He was fully aware of what was happening around him, and he appeared terrified. But I knew him well. His terror wasn't for himself, it was for me. My happiness and safety were his priorities. That was something that would never change. However, it went both ways. His happiness and safety were my goals as well.

"Satisfied?" Fake Bob queried.

"What happened to you?" I asked. The question wasn't to get a rise out of It. I asked in all seriousness.

"I don't know what you mean," It replied.

"Well, I sure do, you Fake Bob Barker, idiot asscrack," Gram yelled, wagging her finger at It. "What my granddaughter asked you was who peed in your soup? Here you are up in some messed up plane with horny game show hosts and weird-ass rules. This is givin' me a real burr in my saddle. Not to mention, you've desecrated the sexiest man alive. You don't hold a candle to Bob Barker, and you should be ashamed of yourself for stealin' his face."

The Higher Power wasn't quite sure what to do. It was probably a once in a very long lifetime event for It.

Gram was on a roll and not even close to being done. "You wanna know what you are? You wanna know? I'm gonna tell you! You're as worthless as gum on a bootheel. You're so full of yourself, you think the sun comes up just to hear you crow. It don't. Sitting up here all high and mighty is about as useless as a steering wheel on a dang mule. You need to get your sorry ass down to the earthly plane and learn some damned manners, shit for brains. There ain't no tear in the Light. You just stole some innocent souls to get Daisy on up here. That makes my butt itch. Guess you weren't expectin' her to have backup," Gram yelled. "Welp, you guessed wrong. I'd suggest you hand over Steve and put your sorry ass into time-out for a few million years."

"Are you done?" It asked, seething with rage.

"Are you?" she shot back.

"Not quite," It replied, pulling Itself back together. "While some of your verbal lashing was right on the money, some was not."

"You wanna be more specific?" I asked.

Its eyes went to Alana Catherine. The expression Its face was a combination of fury and confusion. I didn't like it.

"The old woman was wrong."

"About?" Alana Catherine asked.

"About Daisy coming with backup. I planned it this way," It answered with a tight smile.

That wasn't welcome news, but while It seemed to be doling out information, I was going to press for more. "So, there's no rip in the Light?"

"There is no rip in the Light," It confirmed, Its eyes still glued to Alana Catherine. "What say you we make a deal, Angel of Mercy?"

"We're on the wrong set for that game," I retorted flatly.

It glanced around and then snapped Its fingers. We were now on the set of *Let's Make A Deal*. It was no longer Fake Bob Barker. It was now Fake Monty Hall. For a brief and unhinged moment, I wondered what the real façade of the Higher Power looked like, then laughed. That wasn't important to anything going on. It seemed to have no real identity. From what I'd learned, It took on many different visages. It must suck to have no sense of self and be dependent on the imagination of others.

Not my problem.

"Is this backdrop better?" It asked.

"No, but state your terms," I told It.

"I'm willing to make a trade," It said. "You can have the ghost. I will trade him for Alana Catherine."

"Are you fucking out of your mind?" I shouted at the same time Steve uttered the identical words.

The Higher Power whipped around and glared at Steve. Steve glared right back. It was clear that he believed he had nothing to lose and was going to defend me and my daughter until the end. But he had a lot to lose. The Higher Power could reduce him to dust. It would mean he would be nothing. No more. Just… gone. That was wrong and it wasn't happening on my watch.

The Higher Power would come back if I ended It. I would come back if It ended me. I let my rage back in. The only person who had no chance of coming back was Steve. That was beyond the pale and not on my agenda. Running on emotions could be detrimental, but this time I'd use it to my benefit.

"I don't like you," It snarled at Steve.

"Back at you," Steve said.

The Higher Power let out a growl that made the hair on the back of my neck stand up. When It raised Its hands over Its head, I took my opening. It was going down.

But someone beat me to the punch… kind of.

Alana Catherine let out a piercing scream. It shattered every light on the sound stage. It also blew the roof off the building. Sunlight spilled and illuminated the set. The warmth and beauty of the light was in stark juxtaposition to what was happening.

My daughter raised her hands high then slashed them down to her sides with another scream. Everything went still. Everything except my daughter, Gram, Steve and me. Fake Monty Hall aka the Higher Power was frozen as well. How powerful was my daughter?

"What in tarnation did you just do, Alana Catherine?" Gram asked in a whisper. "Right near lost my hearin.'"

"Umm… I froze time," she whispered back. "Not sure how long it will last. We need to save Steve. Now."

She sprinted up onto the stage with Gram and me on her heels.

"Wait," Steve said as Alana Catherine went to touch him. He smiled at her and studied her face. "I want to meet you properly."

"She's my daughter," I told him.

His smile grew wider, and tears filled his eyes. "She's so beautiful," he said with reverence. "Just like her mom and dad."

"Thank you," I told him. "She's my everything."

"As she should be," he replied, still staring with true delight at Alana Catherine. "I don't think you should save me. It might enrage that thing."

"You ain't suggestin' we make the trade?" Gram asked, confused.

"Never in a million years," Steve told her. "I think you three should just leave if you can. Get out of this place and leave me here. Maybe, that thing will be satisfied with destroying me and leave you alone."

"It won't," Alana Catherine said. "For some reason It wants me. This entire situation was to get me here."

"It can't have you," I ground out.

"Correct," she replied. "But we need to know why It wants me. If we don't we'll be in danger for a very long time, considering how long we live."

"It gives me a nasty butt rash to agree with the little gal, but I do," Gram admitted. "I mean, I'm talkin' a red, raw, in need of medication kind of butt rash."

I blew out a wildly frustrated audible breath. "We get the

picture, Gram. And while I don't completely disagree, I don't think three of us are enough to fight It."

"With all due respect, Mom... I disagree with you. Three is the magic number. We're the past, the present and the future." She then recited what she'd told Pandora. "The game is a riddle. Three must play to win and break the evil spells. The show will go on, and the wheels will turn. The answers are questions. The price must be right, or the innocent will pay. In the end, the choice will be on the strongest. The strongest shall emerge the victor. Anything is possible. You just have to believe. Time is running out."

We listened to the words. We'd already successfully worked our way through most of what was turning out to be a prophecy. None of us could have done it alone. Three was indeed the magic number.

"We are the strongest," Alana Catherine said. "Together, we're the strongest and will emerge as the victor if we believe." She let her gaze meet each of ours. "I believe."

Gram dropped three F-bombs much to Steve's surprise, then took Alana Catherine's hand. "I believe."

They both looked at me. My motherly instincts were warring with my instincts for what was right and what was wrong. I knew in my mind my daughter was right. I just had to get my heart on the same page. I closed my eyes and inhaled deeply. Anything was possible. Anything. I just had to believe. I believed in right over wrong. I believed in justice. I believed in Gideon, Candy Vargo, Heather, Tim, Charlie and the others. I believed in Gram. And what didn't come as a surprise to me at all... I believed in Alana Catherine.

Opening my eyes, I smiled at the two women who were the most important females in my life. "I believe."

"Yes!" Steve yelled. "I believe in all of you! Kick that thing's ass!"

Alana Catherine laughed and extended her arms to Steve. "I want to thank you," she told him.

"For what?" he asked, perplexed.

"For loving my mom. For being her best friend and husband when she was alone. I wouldn't be here if it weren't for you and your journey with my mom. You're such a beautiful soul, Steve. It would be my honor to give you a safe haven inside me until we can bring you back to the Light where you belong."

There wasn't a dry eye in the house.

"Come to me," Alana Catherine urged. "Let me take care of you like you took care of my mom."

Steve was overcome with emotion and nodded jerkily. With a quick and sweet kiss to both Gram and me, he went into my daughter's open arms and disappeared.

"It's time," she stated. "The spell is about to wear off."

"New catchphrase," Gram said. "It's kinda long, but it works... In the end the choice will be on the strongest. The strongest shall emerge the victor. Anything is possible. You just have to believe."

I grinned. It was long past time to end the game.

CHAPTER FIFTEEN

WHEN ALANA CATHERINE'S FREEZE SPELL WORE OFF, THE
Higher Power flew into a rage. It destroyed the entire soundstage with a flick of Its finger, then shrieked so loudly the rest
of the building fell around us. I covered my daughter and
Gram to protect them from a large beam crashing toward us,
but in a poof, it disappeared. The wreckage of the game show
set began to morph and transform until it turned into a stun-
ningly gorgeous field in a valley of wildflowers. It was surreal.

The beauty of the surroundings clashed with the fury of the
being who resided on this plane.

"You shall pay," It snarled. "None of you will leave this
place. Ever. You fucked around and you're about to find out."

"No," Alana Catherine said. "You're wrong."

The Higher Power was taken aback at her words. It was
crazy, but I thought I saw fear for a brief moment in Its eyes.
That had to be wrong. Why would It be afraid of us?

"I. Am. Never. Wrong," It snapped. "My word is the law.
They've been written in stone, and a little half-breed girl can't
subvert her way around them." It laughed menacingly. The

sound shook the entire plane. "I made the laws, and I'm the only one allowed to break them."

"I call bullshit," she said. Alana Catherine clapped her hands. An ancient book appeared. It floated in the air in front of her. The Higher Power gasped. Its eyes narrowed to slits, and It punched a hole in the ground that created a huge crater.

Crap. The divide was vast, and getting over it was going to be a challenge.

Gram grabbed my hand. "Daisy girl," she whispered. "I know that there book. I seen Heather use it."

"What? What are you talking about?"

"I'm thinkin' it's the Immortal Book of Law," she said, sounding a little frantic.

That was nothing. My stomach was one big painful cramp. "Why does Alana Catherine have it?" I asked under my breath.

"Goin' out on a limb here, but I'm gonna say our little gal might be the future Arbitrator Between the Darkness and the Light."

I looked at her askance. How was that even possible?

When the skunks flew out of my daughter one by one, the Higher Power backed up a bit. Even though the crater was a barrier, he wasn't pleased that the skunks had shown up. I recalled Alana Catherine's words—Spiritually, skunks symbolize fearlessness, protection and balance. The black and white of their fur embodies the balance between the dark and the light... Was the Higher Power afraid that Its careless disregard of balance was going to bite It in the ass? Did the skunks come out of my child to remind It of that?

The adorable little stinkers were armed to the butt. They surrounded my daughter in protection. I wish I could say that it gave me a sense of peace, but it didn't calm me at all. Not one little bit. I'd watched them get decimated by a machine gun-wielding Fake Vanna White less than an hour ago. What could they do against a being that created life as we knew it?

Again, I felt like I was in the middle of a fever dream. This didn't look like it was going to end well. Mentally, I gauged the distance that It was standing from me. Alana Catherine's safety was my biggest concern. She was powerful, but how could someone who was a freaking baby this morning, fight the Higher Power with a book and a bunch of cute mammals? She couldn't. However, I could kill the bastard and get us out of here. Jumping the crater was a little iffy, but I was fast. If I got up enough speed, I could make it.

"Gram, when I say go, I want you to cuss like you've never cussed before."

"You want it worse than the string of words I strung together a little while ago?"

I glanced over at her. "You can be nastier than that tirade I lived through?"

"Way," she assured me with a thumbs up. "You should hear Candy Vargo in her sleep. It's a hot mess of poop words. I might be old, but I got a memory like a steel trap. I can singe the hair right out of your ears."

That news was frightening and fabulous at the same time. "You're going to distract It. I'm going to kill It. Then we're leaving."

"We takin' the skunks home?" she asked. "I think Alana Catherine will be real dang disappointed if we don't."

"Umm… I wasn't planning on it, but I suppose I could make it work."

"One more quickie," Gram said. "How we gettin' out of here?"

"I'm gonna click my heels three times and say there's no place like home," I told her.

"Works for me," she said.

I sure as hell hoped it worked for all of us.

Seconds before I gave Gram the go-ahead to set the world on fire with her filthy mouth, Alana Catherine spoke. Her voice was loud and clear. Her words were damning. She knew it. Gram knew it. I knew it, and the Higher Power knew it. It trembled with so much outrage, I wondered if It was about to obliterate the entire plane.

"You have broken the laws you created," my child said, pointing at the book. She glowed brightly in every color of the rainbow.

"Well, I'll be," Gram muttered. "I'd put up with all kinds of rain to see a rainbow like that."

"You," Alana Catherine continued, her voice booming through the valley. "You have removed souls from the Light who did no wrong. You pulled them out for your own selfish reasons."

"So what?" the Higher Power snarled. "What do you think you can do about it?"

Alana Catherine was calm, cool and collected. Her skunk army hung on her every word. Their asses were directly aimed at the Higher Power. It was certain a group butt blast wouldn't kill It, but it wouldn't be what anyone would call fun. "It's not what I will do about it. It's what you will do about it. The punishment for your crime is death. You wrote the law. You wrote the punishment. The question that hangs in the balance is what are *you* going to do about it?"

"Nothing," It snarled.

"That's stupid," Gram yelled. "What in tarnation have you been smokin', Fake Monty Hall? Laws are laws. You heard my great-grandbaby. Ain't no one above the dang law. Not even the real Bob Barker. I'm thinkin' it might be time for an

Immortal election. Y'all need to get you a new leader that ain't batshit crazy."

"Fine," It bellowed, causing a harsh wind to whip through the field. "You win this round. Leave my plane."

"And what about the punishment for your crime?" Alana Catherine demanded, not backing down. "If it hadn't been for Gram, my mom and me, the dead would have been reduced to dust. That's in the law book as well. You would have been looking at a double death sentence."

"You," he hissed, looking at my daughter. "You should not exist."

"Why?" I demanded. "Why should my child not exist?"

It refused to answer, but It still had something to say. Assholes loved to hear themselves talk. It was the OG of assholes. "Unnatural things should be destroyed. Abominations should not exist. EVER."

Are you fucking kidding me?" I shouted back, infuriated that the disgusting waste of space had just called my daughter an abomination. "None of us are natural. We're Immortal. That's not natural. My daughter is a miracle. She will be anything she wants to be and I will support her."

"Put that in your pipe and smoke it, turdknocker!" Gram yelled. "Along with all the crack you've obviously been chewing on."

"Umm... I think people smoke crack," I told her.

"Whatever," Gram said. "That loser got the meanin'."

And apparently Alana Catherine did as well...

"Oh my gosh," she cried out. "I know. I know why you want me so badly. You want—"

"NO," It shrieked, completely losing Its shit. "Whatever you think is wrong. LEAVE MY PLANE!"

The explosions were violent. They rocked the plane and set

the field aflame. I grabbed Gram and sprinted for my daughter. Without missing a beat, Alana Catherine extended her arms to the furry creatures and they dove back into her. That solved the problem of how to get them home. The next issue on the list was if clicking my heels together three times was going to work. The flames were searing hot and coming at us fast. Wrapping my arms around Gram and Alana Catherine, I clicked my heels together three times.

"There's no place like home," I shouted.

Nothing. We were still in the middle of the inferno.

"There's no place like home," I shouted again.

Nothing.

Alana Catherine looked at me like I'd lost my mind. She wasn't far off.

"I've got this, Mom," she said with a smile. "Hang on. We're going home."

THE GREAT ROOM IN MY HOME LOOKED EXACTLY THE SAME AS when we left it. What wasn't the same was me. I would never be the same again after that trip. I was so grateful to be back home surrounded by the people I loved and who loved me back. It felt as if we'd been gone for years.

It had only been a day.

Gram was a ghost again, and my beautiful daughter was a baby. Explaining what had happened was going to take a hot minute, and I was exhausted. Alana Catherine slept soundly in my arms. Part of me would miss the badass version of my daughter. But she'd get there again in twenty years. I was going to enjoy every second of her precious life until then.

Gideon looked as if he'd aged a few centuries, but since he

was older than dirt, he was still beautiful to me, even with his bloodshot eyes and drained expression.

"Here's the fuckin' deal," Candy Vargo said, taking over.

I'd really missed her. I couldn't wait until she heard about Gram's new and horrifying vocabulary. They both were going to need some bathroom and soap time together.

"Daisy needs to sleep," Candy went on. "None of us are goin' nowhere. Mail boy, get the rest of the fuckers back here. We'll debrief everybody at the same time."

"On it," Tim said, pulling out his cellphone.

"You're okay? Really okay?" Gideon questioned. He hadn't stopped touching Alana Catherine and me since we'd arrived home.

The shocker was that our bodies left the earthly plane when we went to the Higher Power's plane. No one was used to that. When I dove into the minds of the dead, my body stayed here. Gideon had lost his mind. He'd even put a call into Cecily to suss out if that had happened with her. It had.

"I'm fine," I promised. It wasn't a lie. Being with my husband and my child was the only place I wanted to be.

"Umm... Daisy," Tim said, pointing at my sleeping baby. "You might want to check that."

I looked down and gasped. Alana Catherine's eyes were still closed, but there was an angelic smile on her pink lips. She was glowing gold. Her small body grew warm and she giggled in her sleep. One by one, the ghosts left their safe haven in the body of the future Soul Keeper. Sam, Birdie, John, Agnes, Sister Catherine and Steve hovered in the air above my miracle child. If I had a feather, I could have knocked Gideon over. He looked like he'd been hit by a truck. I'd explain later. I wasn't about to miss the magic of what was about to go down.

Each of the dead kissed my daughter. After, they took turns

kissing me. It felt so right. En masse, they floated toward the golden light that had appeared in the doorway. Silently and with smiles on their faces each went into the Light and faded away. Everyone was gone but one lone ghost. Steve. It didn't surprise me. I secretly wished he'd stick around for a bit, but I knew he had to go. Steve wrapped his ghostly arms around me, Gideon and Alana Catherine.

"Love each other well," he whispered. "I'll love all three of you from afar. Thank you, Daisy, for saving me in so many ways. Thank you, Gideon, for saving Daisy. And you, little one," he said, caressing Alana Catherine's cheek. Her smile grew wider as she slept. "You are so special. You will always be loved... from here and from the Light. Be the badass, little girl. We need you."

With one last smile that warmed my heart, he floated into the Light. It was the second time I watched him leave me. The first time was hard. This time, it was glorious.

My baby slept through the entire scene. I wondered when all the skunks decided to come out how Gideon would react. We'd have to wait and see...

Glancing up, I winced. Jennifer, Mr. Jackson, Lura Belle, Dimple and Jolly Sue were watching the Game Show Channel. I was pretty sure I never wanted to see a freaking game show again for the rest of my years. Even Gram avoided the television. I hated that the High Power had soured her love for Bob Barker. Another reason to hate the petty Bitch with a capital B.

The TV went fuzzy and made a few popping sounds. Candy Vargo was instantly armed to the teeth. Charlie and Tim began glowing and ushered everyone away from the TV. Gideon's eyes burned red, and he stood protectively in front of Alana Catherine and me.

The picture on the screen slowly came into focus. It took a

minute to realize what we were looking at. Gram gasped and spewed out a litany of cuss words that made Candy Vargo almost pass out. It was so unexpected that Jennifer grabbed a bottle of wine and chugged it.

The faces of Bob Barker and Monty Hall filled the screen. It was an extreme close up and you could see every pore on their faces. It was grotesque.

"That ain't Bob and Monty," Gram hissed. "It's Fake Bob and Fake Monty."

"What the hell did you just say, Gram?" Candy Vargo asked, clearly concerned for Gram's mental state.

"My fuckin' bad," Gram said, smacking herself in the forehead. Candy Vargo's mouth hung open like a fish out of water. "It's the Higher Power. Both of 'em are."

Everyone in the room thought Gram had gone and lost her mind. She had not.

"She's correct," I said flatly. "Turn it up. Let's hear what the Asshole has to say."

Tim did, and we waited.

The two talking heads spoke at the same time and in unison. It was eerie and wrong. "The abomination shall be destroyed. Don't try to fight it. If you do, It will bring on the end."

The screen faded to black.

"What the actual fuck?" Candy Vargo shouted, glowing bright orange. "Somebody wanna explain that?"

Between Gram and me, it took us two hours to get everyone up to speed. Heather, Missy, Tory, my Angel siblings, Zander and Catriona along with our human buddies, June and Amelia, arrived about halfway through and got the gist of it.

"And so," I concluded, "the Higher Power was ready to do

some dastardly crap, but then Alana Catherine said she knew what It wanted, and without warning It tried to burn us alive."

"Okay," Candy Vargo said, chewing on ten toothpicks. "The answer to this is to figure out what Alana Catherine was going to say. It sounds like the Higher Fucker wants her... or is afraid of her for some reason. A reason that your daughter, for some reason, knows."

"Problem is she can't speak," I pointed out, as my body filled with dread.

"There might be a way," Gideon said, but he didn't look confident.

"I'll take any suggestions at this point," I told him.

His jaw clenched. "For too long, the Immortals have ignored the unethical ways of the Higher Power, giving It a wide berth out of fear that It could truly bring the end of us, but I think it's high time our kind joined forces to stop the creator before It does any more damage."

"I'm fuckin' with you," Candy Vargo said. "Besides, I've been around a long time. Getting turned to dust won't be the worst thing to happen to me."

"No one's turning to dust," I stated, my voice higher than usual. "It won't come to that." At least, I hoped it wouldn't. I just had to believe, right?

The one thing I knew for sure... the Higher Power was after our baby. Even if we wanted to avoid the fight, we couldn't. We had no choice. Teaming up to face the ultimate being was a means to an end. Possibly the end of the Higher Power. Possibly the end of us and the universe as we knew it. Either way, we were about to find out. If the creator was after my daughter, I would go after It and make It pay.

"We'll make It pay," Gideon said, reading my mind. "And if

we have to, we'll create a new world if that's what it takes to keep our baby safe."

"May the strongest win," Gram said.

"The strongest will win," I assured her.

There was no other option. For my baby girl, I would keep the faith. I would remind myself that anything was possible as long as I believed.

The End... for now

EXCERPT: THE WRITE HOOK

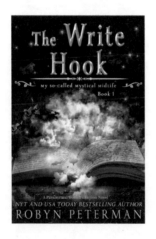

BOOK DESCRIPTION

THE WRITE HOOK

Midlife is full of surprises. Not all of them are working for me.

At forty-two I've had my share of ups and downs. Relatively normal, except when the definition of normal changes... drastically.

NYT Bestselling Romance Author: Check
Amazing besties: Check
Lovely home: Check
Pet cat named Thick Stella who wants to kill me: Check
Wacky Tabacky Dealing Aunt: Check
Cheating husband banging the weather girl on our kitchen table: Check
Nasty Divorce: Oh yes
Characters from my novels coming to life: Umm... yes
Crazy: Possibly

Four months of wallowing in embarrassed depression should

be enough. I'm beginning to realize that no one is who they seem to be, and my life story might be spinning out of my control. It's time to take a shower, put on a bra, and wear something other than sweatpants. Difficult, but doable.

With my friends—real and imaginary—by my side, I need to edit my life before the elusive darkness comes for all of us.

The plot is no longer fiction. It's my reality, and I'm writing a happy ever after no matter what. I just have to find the *write hook*.

CHAPTER 1

"I didn't leave that bowl in the sink," I muttered to no one as I stared in confusion at the blue piece of pottery with milk residue in the bottom. "Wait. Did I?"

Slowly backing away, I ran my hands through my hair that hadn't seen a brush in days—possibly longer—and decided that I wasn't going to think too hard about it. Thinking led to introspective thought, which led to dealing with reality, and that was a no-no.

Reality wasn't my thing right now.

Maybe I'd walked in my sleep, eaten a bowl of cereal, then politely put the bowl in the sink. It was possible.

"That has to be it," I announced, walking out of the kitchen and avoiding all mirrors and any glass where I could catch a glimpse of myself.

It was time to get to work. Sadly, books didn't write themselves.

"I can do this. I have to do this." I sat down at my desk and made sure my posture didn't suck. I was fully aware it would suck in approximately five minutes, but I wanted to start out right. It would be a bad week to throw my back out. "Today, I'll write ten thousand words. They will be coherent. I will not mistakenly or on purpose make a list of the plethora of ways I would like to kill Darren. He's my past. Beheading him is illegal. I'm far better than that. On a more positive note, my imaginary muse will show his ponytailed, obnoxious ass up today, and I won't play Candy Jelly Crush until the words are on the page."

Two hours later...

Zero words. However, I'd done three loads of laundry—sweatpants, t-shirts and underwear—and played Candy Jelly Crush until I didn't have any more lives. As pathetic as I'd become, I hadn't sunk so low as to purchase new lives. That would mean I'd hit rock bottom. Of course, I was precariously close, evidenced by my cussing out of the Jelly Queen for ten minutes, but I didn't pay for lives. I considered it a win.

I'd planned on folding the laundry but decided to vacuum instead. I'd fold the loads by Friday. It was Tuesday. That was reasonable. If they were too wrinkled, I'd simply wash them again. No biggie. After the vacuuming was done, I rearranged my office for thirty minutes. I wasn't sure how to Feng Shui, but after looking it up on my phone, I gave it a half-assed effort.

Glancing around at my handiwork, I nodded. "Much better. If the surroundings are aligned correctly, the words will flow magically. I hope."

Two hours later...

"Mother humper," I grunted as I pushed my monstrosity of a bed from one side of the bedroom to the other. "This weighs a damn ton."

I'd burned all the bedding seven weeks ago. The bonfire had been cathartic. I'd taken pictures as the five hundred thread count sheets had gone up in flame. I'd kept the comforter. I'd paid a fortune for it. It had been thoroughly saged and washed five times. Even though there was no trace of Darren left in the bedroom, I'd been sleeping in my office.

The house was huge, beautiful… and mine—a gorgeously restored Victorian where I'd spent tons of time as a child. It had an enchanted feel to it that I adored. I didn't need such an enormous abode, but I loved the location—the middle of nowhere. The internet was iffy, but I solved that by going into town to the local coffee shop if I had something important to download or send.

Darren, with the wandering pecker, thought he would get a piece of the house. He was wrong. I'd inherited it from my whackadoo grandmother and great-aunt Flip. My parents hadn't always been too keen on me spending so much time with Granny and Aunt Flip growing up, but I adored the two old gals so much they'd relented. Since I spent a lot of time in an imaginary dream world, my mom and dad were delighted when I related to actual people—even if they were left of center.

Granny and Flip made sure the house was in my name only —nontransferable and non-sellable. It was stipulated that I had to pass it to a family member or the Historical Society when I died. Basically, I had life rights. It was as if Granny and Aunt Flip had known I would waste two decades of my life married to a jackhole who couldn't keep his salami in his pants and would need someplace to live. God rest Granny's insane soul. Aunt Flip was still kicking, although I hadn't seen her in a few years.

Aunt Flip put the K in kooky. She'd bought a cottage in the hills about an hour away and grew medicinal marijuana— before it was legal. The old gal was the black sheep of the family and preferred her solitude and her pot to company. She hadn't liked Darren a bit. She and Granny both had worn black to my wedding. Everyone had been appalled—even me—but in the end, it made perfect sense. I had to hand it to the old broads. They'd been smarter than me by a long shot. And the house? It had always been my charmed haven in the storm.

Even though there were four spare bedrooms plus the master suite, I chose my office. It felt safe to me.

Thick Stella preferred my office, and I needed to be around something that had a heartbeat. It didn't matter that Thick Stella was bitchy and swiped at me with her deadly kitty claws every time I passed her. I loved her. The feeling didn't seem mutual, but she hadn't left me for a twenty-three-year-old with silicone breast implants and huge, bright white teeth.

"Thick Stella, do you think Sasha should wear red to her stepmother's funeral?" I asked as I plopped down on my newly Feng Shuied couch and narrowly missed getting gouged by my cat. "Yes or no? Hiss at me if it's a yes. Growl at me if it's a no."

Thick Stella had a go at her privates. She was useless.

"That wasn't an answer." I grabbed my laptop from my desk. Deciding it was too dangerous to sit near my cat, I settled for the love seat. The irony of the piece of furniture I'd chosen didn't escape me.

"I think she should wear red," I told Thick Stella, who didn't give a crap what Sasha wore. "Her stepmother was an asshat, and it would show fabu disrespect."

Typing felt good. Getting lost in a story felt great. I dressed Sasha in a red Prada sheath, then had her behead her ex-husband with a dull butter knife when he and his bimbo showed up unexpectedly to pay their respects at the funeral home. It was a bloodbath. Putting Sasha in red was an excellent move. The blood matched her frock to a T.

Quickly rethinking the necessary murder, I moved the scene of the decapitation to the empty lobby of the funeral home. It would suck if I had to send Sasha to prison. She hadn't banged Damien yet, and everyone was eagerly awaiting the sexy buildup—including me. It was the fourth book in the series, and it was about time they got together. The sexual tension was palpable.

"What in the freaking hell?" I snapped my laptop shut and groaned. "Sasha doesn't have an ex-husband. I can't do this. I've got nothing." Where was my muse hiding? I needed the elusive imaginary idiot if I was going to get any writing done. "Chauncey, dammit, where are you?"

"My God, you're loud, Clementine," a busty, beautiful woman dressed in a deep purple Regency gown said with an eye roll.

She was seated on the couch next to Thick Stella, who barely acknowledged her. My cat attacked strangers and friends. Not today. My fat feline simply glanced over at the intruder and yawned. The cat was a traitor.

Forget the furry betrayer. How in the heck did the woman get into my house—not to mention my office—without me seeing her enter? For a brief moment, I wondered if she'd banged my husband too but pushed the sordid thought out of my head. She looked to be close to thirty—too old for the asshole.

"Who are you?" I demanded, holding my laptop over my head as a weapon.

If I threw it and it shattered, I would be screwed. I couldn't remember the last time I'd backed it up. If I lost the measly, somewhat disjointed fifty thousand words I'd written so far, I'd have to start over. That wouldn't fly with my agent or my publisher.

"Don't be daft," the woman replied. "It's rather unbecoming. May I ask a question?"

"No, you may not," I shot back, trying to place her.

She was clearly a nutjob. The woman was rolling up on thirty but had the vernacular of a seventy-year-old British society matron. She was dressed like she'd walked off the set of a film starring Emma Thompson. Her blonde hair shone to the point of absurdity and was twisted into an elaborate up-do. Wispy tendrils framed her perfectly heart-shaped face. Her sparkling eyes were lavender, enhanced by the over-the-top gown she wore.

Strangely, she was vaguely familiar. I just couldn't remember how I knew her.

"How long has it been since you attended to your hygiene?" she inquired.

Putting my laptop down and picking up a lamp, I eyed her. I didn't care much for the lamp or her question. I had been thinking about Marie Condo-ing my life, and the lamp didn't bring me all that much joy. If it met its demise by use of self-defense, so be it. "I don't see how that's any of your business, lady. What I'd suggest is that you leave. Now. Or else I'll call the police. Breaking and entering is a crime."

She laughed. It sounded like freaking bells. Even though she was either a criminal or certifiable, she was incredibly charming.

"Oh dear," she said, placing her hand delicately on her still heaving, milky-white bosom. "You are so silly. The constable knows quite well that I'm here. He advised me to come."

"The constable?" I asked, wondering how far off her rocker she was.

She nodded coyly. "Most certainly. We're all terribly concerned."

I squinted at her. "About my hygiene?"

"That, amongst other things," she confirmed. "Darling girl, you are not an ace of spades or, heaven forbid, an adventuress. Unless you want to be an ape leader, I'd recommend bathing."

"Are you right in the head?" I asked, wondering where I'd left my damn cell phone. It was probably in the laundry room. I was going to be murdered by a nutjob, and I'd lost my chance to save myself because I'd been playing Candy Jelly Crush. The headline would be horrifying—*Homeless-looking, Hygiene-free Paranormal Romance Author Beheaded by Victorian Psycho.*

If I lived through the next hour, I was deleting the game for good.

"I think it would do wonders for your spirit if you donned a nice tight corset and a clean chemise," she suggested, skillfully ignoring my question. "You must pull yourself together. Your behavior is dicked in the nob."

I sat down and studied her. My about-to-be-murdered radar relaxed a tiny bit, but I kept the lamp clutched tightly in my hand. My gut told me she wasn't going to strangle me. Of course, I could be mistaken, but Purple Gal didn't seem violent —just bizarre. Plus, the lamp was heavy. I could knock her ladylike ass out with one good swing.

How in the heck did I know her? College? Grad School? The grocery store? At forty-two, I'd met a lot of people in my life. Was she with the local community theater troop? I was eighty-six percent sure she wasn't here to off me. However, I'd been wrong about life-altering events before—like not knowing my husband was boffing someone young enough to have been our daughter.

"What language are you speaking?" I spotted a pair of scissors on my desk. If I needed them, it was a quick move to grab them. I'd never actually killed anyone except in fictitious situations, but there was a first time for everything.

Pulling an embroidered lavender hankey from her cleavage, she clutched it and twisted it in her slim fingers. "Clementine, *you* should know."

"I'm at a little disadvantage here," I said, fascinated by the batshit crazy woman who'd broken into my home. "You seem to know my name, but I don't know yours."

And that was when the tears started. Hers. Not mine.

"Such claptrap. How very unkind of you, Clementine," she burst out through her stupidly attractive sobs.

It was ridiculous how good the woman looked while crying. I got all blotchy and red, but not the mystery gal in purple. She grew even more lovely. It wasn't fair. I still had no clue what the hell she was talking about, but on the off chance she might throw a tantrum if I asked more questions, I kept my mouth shut.

And yes, she had a point, but my *hygiene* was none of her damn business. I couldn't quite put my finger on the last time I'd showered. If I had to guess, it was probably in the last five to twelve days. I was on a deadline for a book. To be more precise, I was late for my deadline on a book. I didn't exactly have time for personal sanitation right now.

And speaking of deadlines…

"How about this?" My tone was excessively polite. I almost laughed. The woman had illegally entered my house, and I was behaving like she was a guest. "I'll take a shower later today after I get through a few pivotal chapters. Right now, you should leave so I can work."

"Yes, of course," she replied, absently stroking Fat Stella, who purred. If I'd done that, I would be minus a finger. "It would be dreadfully sad if you were under the hatches."

I nodded. "Right. That would, umm… suck."

The woman in purple smiled. It was radiant, and I would have sworn I heard birds happily chirping. I was losing it.

"Excellent," she said, pulling a small periwinkle velvet bag from her cleavage. I wondered what else she had stored in there and hoped there wasn't a weapon. "I shall leave you with two gold coins. While the Grape Nuts were tasty, I would prefer that you purchase some Lucky Charms. I understand they are magically delicious."

"It was you?" I asked, wildly relieved that I hadn't been sleep eating. I had enough problems at the moment. Gaining weight from midnight dates with cereal wasn't on the to-do list.

"It was," she confirmed, getting to her feet and dropping the coins into my hand. "The consistency was quite different from porridge, but I found it tasty—very crunchy."

"Right… well… thank you for putting the bowl in the sink." Wait. Why the hell was I thanking her? She'd wandered in and eaten my Grape Nuts.

"You are most welcome, Clementine," she said with a disarming smile that lit up her unusual eyes. "It was lovely finally meeting you even if your disheveled outward show is entirely astonishing."

I was reasonably sure I had just been insulted by the cereal lover, but it was presented with excellent manners. However, she did answer a question. We hadn't met. I wasn't sure why she seemed familiar. The fact that she knew my name was alarming.

"Are you a stalker?" I asked before I could stop myself.

I'd had a few over the years. Being a *New York Times* best-selling author was something I was proud of, but it had come with a little baggage here and there. Some people seemed to have difficulty discerning fiction from reality. If I had to guess, I'd say Purple Gal might be one of those people.

I'd only written one Regency novel, and that had been at the beginning of my career, before I'd found my groove in paranormal romance. I was way more comfortable writing about demons and vampires than people dressed in top hats and hoopskirts. Maybe the crazy woman had read my first book. It hadn't done well, and for good reason. It was over-the-top bad. I'd blocked the entire novel out of my mind. Live and learn. It had been my homage to Elizabeth Hoyt well over a decade ago. It had been clear to all that I should leave Regency romance to the masters.

"Don't be a Merry Andrew," the woman chided me. "Your bone box is addled. We must see to it at once. I shall pay a visit again soon."

The only part of her gibberish I understood was that she thought she was coming back. Note to self—change all the locks on the doors. Since it wasn't clear if she was packing heat in her cleavage, I just smiled and nodded.

"Alrighty then…" I was unsure if I should walk her to the door or if she would let herself out. Deciding it would be better to make sure she actually left instead of letting her hide in my pantry to finish off my cereal, I gestured to the door. "Follow me."

Thick Stella growled at me. I was so tempted to flip her off but thought it might earn another lecture from Purple Gal. It was more than enough to be lambasted for my appearance. I didn't need my manners picked apart by someone with a tenuous grip on reality.

My own grip was dubious as it was.

"You might want to reconsider breaking into homes," I said, holding the front door open. "It could end badly—for you."

Part of me couldn't believe that I was trying to help the nutty woman out, but I couldn't seem to stop myself. I kind of liked her.

"I'll keep that in mind," she replied as she sauntered out of my house into the warm spring afternoon. "Remember, Clementine, there is always sunshine after the rain."

As she made her way down the long sunlit, tree-lined drive, she didn't look back. It was disturbingly like watching the end of a period movie where the heroine left her old life behind and walked proudly toward her new and promising future.

Glancing around for a car, I didn't spot one. Had she left it parked on the road so she could make a clean getaway after she'd bludgeoned me? Had I just politely escorted a murderer out of my house?

Had I lost it for real?

Probably.

As she disappeared from sight, I felt the weight of the gold coins still clutched in my hand. Today couldn't get any stranger.

At least, I hoped not.

Opening my fist to examine the coins, I gasped. "What in the heck?"

There was nothing in my hand.

Had I dropped them? Getting down on all fours, I searched. Thick Stella joined me, kind of—more like watched me as I crawled around and wondered if anything that had just happened had actually happened.

"Purple Gal gave me coins to buy Lucky Charms," I told my cat, my search now growing frantic. "You saw her do it. Right? She sat next to you. And you didn't attack her. *Right?*"

Thick Stella simply stared at me. What did I expect? If my cat answered me, I'd have to commit myself. That option might still be on the table. Had I just imagined the entire exchange with the strange woman? Should I call the cops?

"And tell them what?" I asked, standing back up and locking the front door securely. "That a woman in a purple gown broke in and ate my cereal while politely insulting my hygiene? Oh, and she left me two gold coins that disappeared in my hand as soon as she was out of sight? That's not going to work."

I'd call the police if she came back, since I wasn't sure she'd been here at all. She hadn't threatened to harm me. Purple Gal had been charming and well-mannered the entire time she'd badmouthed my cleanliness habits. And to be quite honest, real or not, she'd made a solid point. I could use a shower.

Maybe four months of wallowing in self-pity and only living inside the fictional worlds I created on paper had taken more of a toll than I was aware of. Getting lost in my stories was one of my favorite things to do. It had saved me more than once over the years. It was possible that I'd let it go too far. Hence, the Purple Gal hallucination.

Shit.

First things first. Delete Candy Jelly Crush. Getting rid of the white noise in my life was the first step to... well, the first step to something.

I'd figure it out later.

ROBYN'S BOOK LIST

(IN CORRECT READING ORDER)

<u>HOT DAMNED SERIES</u>
Fashionably Dead
Fashionably Dead Down Under
Hell on Heels
Fashionably Dead in Diapers
A Fashionably Dead Christmas
Fashionably Hotter Than Hell
Fashionably Dead and Wed
Fashionably Fanged
Fashionably Flawed
A Fashionably Dead Diary
Fashionably Forever After
Fashionably Fabulous
A Fashionable Fiasco
Fashionably Fooled
Fashionably Dead and Loving It
Fashionably Dead and Demonic
The Oh My Gawd Couple
A Fashionable Disaster

GOOD TO THE LAST DEMON SERIES
As the Underworld Turns
The Edge of Evil
The Bold and the Banished
Guiding Blight
Blaze of Our Lives

GOOD TO THE LAST DEATH SERIES
It's a Wonderful Midlife Crisis
Whose Midlife Crisis Is It Anyway?
A Most Excellent Midlife Crisis
My Midlife Crisis, My Rules
You Light Up My Midlife Crisis
It's A Matter of Midlife and Death
The Facts Of Midlife
It's A Hard Knock Midlife
Run for Your Midlife
It's A Hell of A Midlife

MY SO-CALLED MYSTICAL MIDLIFE SERIES
The Write Hook
You May Be Write
All The Write Moves
My Big Fat Hairy Wedding

SHIFT HAPPENS SERIES
Ready to Were
Some Were in Time
No Were To Run
Were Me Out
Were We Belong

MAGIC AND MAYHEM SERIES
Switching Hour
Witch Glitch
A Witch in Time
Magically Delicious
A Tale of Two Witches
Three's A Charm
Switching Witches
You're Broom or Mine?
The Bad Boys of Assjacket
The Newly Witch Game
Witches In Stitches

SEA SHENANIGANS SERIES
Tallulah's Temptation
Ariel's Antics
Misty's Mayhem
Petunia's Pandemonium
Jingle Me Balls

A WYLDE PARANORMAL SERIES
Beauty Loves the Beast

HANDCUFFS AND HAPPILY EVER AFTERS SERIES
How Hard Can it Be?
Size Matters
Cop a Feel

If after reading all the above you are still wanting more adventure and zany fun, read *Pirate Dave and His Randy Adventures*, the romance novel budding novelist Rena helped wicked Evangeline write in *How Hard Can It Be?*

Warning: Pirate Dave Contains Romance Satire, Spoofing, and
Pirates with Two Pork Swords.

NOTE FROM THE AUTHOR

If you enjoyed reading *Having the Time of My Midlife*, please consider leaving a positive review or rating on the site where you purchased it. Reader reviews help my books continue to be valued by resellers and help new readers make decisions about reading them.

You are the reason I write these stories and I sincerely appreciate each of you!

Many thanks for your support,
~ Robyn Peterman

Want to hear about my new releases?
Visit https://robynpeterman.com/newsletter/ and join my mailing list!

ABOUT ROBYN PETERMAN

Robyn Peterman writes because the people inside her head won't leave her alone until she gives them life on paper. Her addictions include laughing really hard with friends, shoes (the expensive kind), Target, Coke (the drink not the drug LOL) with extra ice in a Yeti cup, bejeweled reading glasses, her kids, her super-hot hubby and collecting stray animals.

A former professional actress with Broadway, film and T.V. credits, she now lives in the South with her family and too many animals to count.

Writing gives her peace and makes her whole, plus having a job where she can work in sweatpants is perfect for her.

Made in the USA
Thornton, CO
12/31/24 11:06:34